The Brave Maiden

The Brave Maiden

By Geoffrey Craig

Acknowledgements:
I would like to acknowledge the fantastic work of Glenn Lyvers and April Zipser of Prolific Press who have done a fabulous job of editing, design, and promotion. The Brave Maiden is the second book of mine they have published, and it was an enormous pleasure to work with them on both occasions.

The Brave Maiden was previously serialized in Wilderness House Literary Review.

The Brave Maiden
©2017 Geoffrey Craig
Cover image: Licensed by Prolific Press Inc.
Published by Prolific Press Inc., Johnstown, PA.
ISBN: 978-1-63275-109-6
Edited by: Glenn Lyvers and April Zipser
Printed in the USA

For Danielle,

with love.

Table of Contents

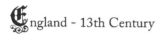

Prologue

England - 13th Century

England, fairest England, cowered in fear;
Doom was forecast by each prophet and seer.
Grim death and hunger roamed all through the land.
Drowned merchants' corpses washed up on the sand
As wild pirates plied their odious trade
And seldom, if ever, were good laws made.
Greed and rank lust begat crimes everywhere;
Taxes were more than poor peasants could bear.
Arrogant knights' weak villages plundered;
From their sacred oaths, their swords were sundered.

Earls and dukes, now a perfidious breed,
Their vassals and liegemen they chose to bleed,
Who, in turn, fastened fat reeves like leeches
On farms and fields, leaving naught but breeches
To humble serfs they were sworn to protect.
This corruption the Church did soon infect.
No longer for victims' sanctuaries,
Chapels amassed gilded reliquaries.
Freebooting knights violated the Mass,
Looting pockets in a manner most crass.

Even poor wayfarers feared for their lives;
And many fell to brigands' cruel knives.
They would cut you for two pence or a pound
And leave your throat gushing blood on the ground.
For a fever that of its own accord
Would have soon vanished like the Golden Horde,
A barber would bleed you with rusted knife,
Then impound your farm including your wife
If you refused to pay his cutthroat fee,
To which in dire panic you did agree.

Justice might be found in the rich squire's court,
Of course, with a bribe with which to resort.
Honor and valor were in short supply;
For the slightest reason, a man could die.
King John sat atop this foul heap of dung,
A villain but wanting his praises sung;
And so, he pretends to great piety
While stealing with all due propriety.
Followed by a cadre of scant regard;
The vilest was a count known as Gerard,

A knight who murdered for gold and pleasure,
His coffers flowing with jeweled treasure.
He confiscates lands without a writ
As the King's right-hand man and favorite.
Peasants huddled in fear when he rode by;
His heart stone, though he hears a baby cry
From hunger because the year's crops had failed.
Next to Gerard, even the devil paled!
His skin mottled, his mouth drawn and thin,
He had a scar that ran from cheek to chin.

Fear caused the serfs to see portents and signs
In breeding stock turned barren and sour wines.
Comets tempted sages to prophecy;
The times brought priests to fetid heresy.
A skulking dog howled at an eclipsed moon;
The dread Apocalypse will follow soon.
Weary scholars cried as they knelt and quaked;
Haggard crones through goats' gory entrails raked.
Men fled to worship in ancient cromlechs
Seeking some relief from moth-eaten texts.

One light shone in this dark night of evil:
A crusading earl both strong and civil
Who sought long and hard for a path of peace
And thought the future lay with King John's niece.
He had a fair daughter whom he adored,

Teaching her early to fight with a sword.
But there was more in this strife-torn nation:
A mystic world of imagination.
Sprites, goblins and elves filled an airy scene
With joyous games led by an elfin Queen.

I

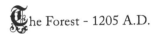The Forest - 1205 A.D.

Dark green shone the forest that April day.
The streams crested their banks along her way.
Swollen drops fell from the thick, mottled trees;
And tender leaves sighed in the fresh spring breeze.
Her cloak felt heavy with the morning dew.
The bright, rising sun struggled to break through
The sodden, grey clouds covering the sky.
She rode tensely, keeping a wary eye,
For in fair England, these were troubled times;
And many fell victim to ghastly crimes.

A pile of leaves her bed the night before,
She rose to her feet feeling wet and sore.
Taking from her pouch a stale crust of bread,
She let cold stream water clear her thick head.
She rode a lean, sure-footed chestnut mare.
They appeared to be an unlikely pair
To travel alone in this fearsome land
Where cutthroats ventured only in a band.
Four weary, hungry days has she traveled
Fleeing from a scene that had unraveled

Her young nerves and left her senses frozen.
To escape death, why had she been chosen?
Finding the bodies lying all around,
She had screamed without uttering a sound.
Wearing doeskin trousers of palest blue,
A soiled doublet and velvet cap askew,
She sat easily in her fine saddle,
Ready to smite any foe in battle.
Hanging from her pommel, a sword at rest;
She wore a dagger with a fancy crest.

She was a slender girl of just sixteen.
Thick auburn hair framed a face tan and lean
And shone brightly as autumn leaves on fire.
She sat as straight as the lonely church spire
Rising near where her Father's castle stood
By a clear river near a game-filled wood.
She recalled that the castle was no more
And the revenge that on her knees she swore,
Kneeling in tears by the newly filled graves
Dug with the help of two loyal Welsh slaves.

Her flashing eyes were the most startling blue.
Her winsome gaze was level, firm and true;
But now fat tears rolled down her slender cheeks,
And her sad face was marked with muddy streaks.
The sun began to warm her chill body.
She smiled a little and thought how shoddy
Her dank clothes must look and how her Mother
Would scold – and how she missed her small brother.
She paused to watch a shaft of intense light
Pierce the thick forest gloom with all its might.

Staring at the spot where the sunlight struck,
She spotted a gleam in the leafy muck.
Her probing fingers found a silver coin.
She groaned as she thought of the juicy loin
Of pork to be bought at the village fair
With several copper pennies to spare.
The coin found a home in her leather pouch.
Hearing a sharp noise, she dropped to a crouch
And touched the crested dagger in her belt.
Something wild was near: not yet seen but felt.

A snarling boar stood not five rods away;
Her skittish mare reared and began to neigh.
The sharp, curving tusks caught the maiden's eye.
"I have a lot to do before I die,"
Ran through her head as she reached for her sword.

The feral beast snorted loudly and pawed
The earth. Pointing her sword towards its snout,
She jiggled her pouch; and the coin fell out.
The charging boar halted as if struck dead,
Turned and through the forest in panic fled.

Picking up the coin, she, for the first time,
Saw symbols that made neither sense nor rhyme.
Putting the magic coin back in its place,
She mounted and set off at a brisk pace.
Her clothes were now dry, but sharp hunger pangs
Attacked her stomach with ravenous fangs
Whose fury a hearty stew could appease.
The crust of bread was but a naughty tease.
She had never thought much on food before;
Plentiful had been the table and more.

Her father was lord of a great fiefdom
Of rich woods and farms in John's broad kingdom.
He was a kindly man though somewhat gruff
Who ensured his loyal serfs had enough
To eat and warm, fustian clothing to wear.
Many other nobles seemed not to care.
To the west lay the broad Blaxford Forest
Whose game added to the autumn harvest.
Northwards, Count Gerard ruled his vast estate
As befits a man of huge greed and hate.

She rode without plan or destination
But just to flee the stark desolation.
The terrified peasants begged her to leave,
Which gave her precious little time to grieve.
Count Gerard, they said, would surely return
To murder her and very likely burn
What little he had last time left behind.
She had taken her morning ride, to find
Returning, the bodies of her parents
And the whole household, not sparing servants.

Kneeling and rocking by her Father's side,
His stiff, lifeless hand, she held fast and cried.
Then she noticed something awfully strange:
His long, blood-stained sword lay just out of range,
But his crested dagger could not be found
Though she searched all over the blood-soaked ground.
This dagger in his belt he always wore;
It was the wellspring of family lore,
Given to each member who learned to fight.
She was the first maiden to earn the right

To wear this family badge of honor.
But she had yet to test her young valor
On the fearful field of mortal combat.
Skilled also with a lance, she firmly sat
Her horse in many a shire tournament.
Facing a determined foe who is bent
On killing you is clearly something else.
Your knees turn to jelly; your stomach melts.
Hard-bitten knights have fled the gory field
Or gotten down on craven knees to yield.

Her thoughts had drifted to a steaming bath
When a scared, little rabbit crossed her path.
Wishing she had been taught to use the bow,
She heard her Father's words almost as though
He was standing there: tall, serene and proud.
She had knelt before him, head slightly bowed.
In a voice that belied his gentle soul,
He described a noble warrior's role:
"The sword is the arm of a war-like race
Followed in turn by hammer, lance and mace.

The bow belongs to our good yeoman friends
Who help our noble purposes and ends."
Her Father took this duty as given:
To bring peace to a land sadly riven
By cutthroat barons and a greedy king.

These vicious murders could mean just one thing,
For evil Gerard was but King John's tool
To perpetuate his inhuman rule.
The count's own objective was far less grand:
Enough for him to be the king's right hand.

Her solemn thoughts were suddenly disturbed
By shrill, jolting insults that flew uncurbed
Through the dense forest and assailed her ears.
She spurred on the mare despite gnawing fears.

II

The Yeoman's Son

"Cursed be ye blasphemous, murdering thieves;
Stay away from me, or you'll see who grieves."
With that, he smote fervently left and right,
Wielding an oaken staff with all his might.
He was a wiry lad with curly hair
And did not seem one to easily scare.
But the fight was not to his advantage;
His bleeding forehead needed a bandage.
Bow and arrows were slung across his back;
On the ground lay an old, disheveled pack.

Three scowling knaves advanced, daggers ready;
She cantered to the fray, sword held steady.
Swinging precisely, she sliced off an ear;
The villain's scream you could easily hear
Halfway across the thickly wooded shire.
The scream only raised her hackles higher:
Another stroke and she dislodged a nose.
This scarred ruffian would no longer pose
A major threat to a traveler's rest.
The cursing, ill-clad rascals thought it best

To take, like screeching magpies, to their heels,
Dodging through the trees like slippery eels.
The young fellow stood and intensely gazed
At this slim girl who was indeed amazed
That her first battle was so quickly done.
My God, she thought, it seems I've really won.
"I could have handled those knaves on my own,"
He said in a surly, complaining tone.
"Of that, I'm quite sure," she gently replied.
"But that I need practice, I cannot hide."

At that, he changed his tone and bowed his head:
"Your servant, milady," he shyly said.
"How well, my new friend, can you shoot that bow?"
A novel idea began to grow.
He smiled a winning smile of jagged teeth
And took an arrow from his ragged sheath.
Duly impressed with an expert display,
Supper, she thought, will soon be on the way.
Munching thereafter on a tender hare,
Seldom could she remember better fare.

She poked a pointed stick into the fire
And thought perhaps a good time to inquire:
"What is your given name? Where are you from?"
"Wales, milady. And my name is William.
Son of honest yeomen and not a serf,
My one aim in life is to prove my worth."
"William the Archer, I wish to call thee;
Of service, sans doute, you will prove to be.
Father taught me the sword, my Mother, French;
But I spent scant time on a student's bench.

I would rather gallop than read a book
Though at a few pages I'll sneak a look.
Dear Mother said that one of high degree
Needs reading, writing and diplomacy,
Not just to sit a horse or swing a sword.
But with my books, I was so often bored."
"Milady, I would fain learn how to read;
We Welsh have always been a fighting breed
And have too long ignored the scholar's art
For which we care not a fig nor a fart."

She nodded and regarded him in turn:
"You as well have a skill that I must learn:
To draw and shoot with yon bow and arrow
Well enough to hit a fleeting sparrow."
Next day William chose a tall, slender yew;

And with fast, deft strokes, he began to hew
A long bow with a supple, arching curve.
He searched for narrow feathers that would serve
To propel her arrows smoothly and straight.
By then the afternoon was growing late,

So, on a broad elm tree, he loosed some bark.
"Milady, pray thee hit that easy mark."
She drew back the bowstring and then let fly.
"Perhaps you'll improve on the second try."
Her arrow had not simply missed the tree;
It had fallen hardly beyond her knee.
He demonstrated how to draw the string
And alongside her cheek two fingers bring.
Her second shot did not come a crupper
So happily, they sat down to supper.

The roasted squirrel was a little tough.
She longed for the old castle cook enough
(With her fragrant herbs and hot, pungent stews)
To sigh ever so quietly and lose
Herself in a far distant reverie.
William chewed his food and watched patiently,
His heart catching fire with a budding love
That came, he surely knew, from God above.
"Your mare," William asked. "Does she have a name?"
"With her bold spirit, she is known as Flame."

"Milady, I wander because our land
Goes to the eldest: though poor - nothing grand.
I have pursued an unsavory way;
An archer finds it hard to earn his pay.
But pray tell me, if I may prove so bold:
What brings a noble maid into this cold,
Unforgiving, dark and frightening wood -
Crowded with spirits that intend no good?"
"Faith, lad, so adept with bow and arrow,
Dost thou fear the merest, flitting shadow?"

A soft, swirling breeze stirred her reddish hair.
A smile graced her lips - from she knew not where.
Just for a moment, she heard a whisper.
Her cheek felt as though someone had kissed her.
Absentmindedly she rubbed at the spot,
Then sternly shook her head. No, it cannot
Be. That's what my dear Father loved to do;
My mind knows how to play a trick or two.
The whispering breeze swirled around once more;
A few leaves rustled on the forest floor.

"All were murdered by a cutthroat baron
Who should be hung like a common felon.
Our castle burnt, my family all killed;
I swore a sacred oath to be fulfilled
When craven Gerard lies dead at my feet.
My avenging fury he will not cheat.
Father long dreamed of a peace enduring.
Yet peace is but a phantom alluring
While the nobles rampage and kill unchecked;
And our lands, and hopes, are cruelly wrecked.

True justice is everywhere over thrown
With evil consequences yet unknown.
Thievery and craven murder abound;
The poor peasants suffer without a sound.
Their children have scarcely enough to eat
When they are shorn of their barley and wheat."
"Brave words, milady, that rightly inspire
And should impel our lords to some higher
Duty. But how says our most worthy King?"
"Our King is found worthy in just one thing:

Levying taxes to increase his wealth.
He cares naught for his wretched people's health."
"What then, milady, can a poor soul do?"
"I wish I knew, William, I wish I knew.
But for now, I pray, let us take our ease

And study this a moment if you please."
Speaking thus, from her leather pouch she drew
A worn book with a cover limned in blue.
"I anticipate, Will, that your first try
Goes further than I made an arrow fly."

With heads bowed together by the firelight,
She gave a lesson from Tales of a Knight.

III

he Tinker

Apollo burst at dawn from his palace,
And Spring painted a riotous canvas
Of blazing flowers and ripening buds.
She chewed cold squirrel as cows chew their cuds.
Her thoughts whirling and her spirits giddy,
She recalled the much-teased antique biddy
Who throughout the year was mean and cranky,
But come spring would wave a faded hanky,
Go half mad and dance on the village green
As if beguiled by a translucent queen.

The nectar of spring has this wild effect,
She thought, and may in us show some defect
That our hearts, which should be forever sad,
Can, with spring's coming, turn foolish and glad.
Brightly clad nature to our minds imparts
A febrile joy, but not peace to our hearts.
Let not memories spoil this sunny day,
But rather mount up and be on our way.
We must find a place in the forest deep
Where we can in due safety live and sleep.

She rode with William walking by her side,
Thinking how he could travel far and wide
And nowhere find such a smart, comely maid;
Nor one who was truly so unafraid
Of the myriad dangers lurking near.
For while young William felt nary a fear
Of any mortal be it man or beast,
The unseen world of spirits never ceased
To fill his mind with wonder and alarm
Though he could never point to any harm

That hobgoblins or pranking elves had caused.
Then in this ambling reverie, he paused
To remember from home the pretty lass
Who burst into twinges one day in mass,
Hopped about and skipped in a crazy dance
And then collapsed on the floor in a trance.
"Jealous wood nymphs," said superstitious folk,
"Cast on her a spell – their malicious joke."
"Blasphemy," said the priest sounding severe.
"Twas due to kissing boys and drinking beer."

"William! Pray, have you heard a single word?
Am I twittering like a silly bird?"
"Yes, milady ... I mean, certainly not,"
Stammered the poor lad as his face grew hot.
"Father, as I was saying, had a plan
That he shared with only one trusted man,
A boon companion and wise magician
Who became counselor and physician."
"Was he not then murdered with all the rest?"
"No, by God's grace, he was traveling west

On a mission to the Welch border earls.
He carried a dozen luminous pearls –
One for each lord to take a solemn pledge
That justice (a right not a privilege)
They would, unto death, uphold with their swords
Thus putting a curb on all wayward lords.
Wouldst that our wise Ormond were here today;
That he remains safe, we can only pray."
They then heard something altogether queer:
A whining voice murmuring words unclear.

Curious, she drew her sword just in case
And rode forward at a slow, cautious pace.
William followed the mare staying close by –
With his oaken staff held firmly and high
Ready to cudgel a threatening foe,

Whether his station be high-born or low.
A few paces on, they saw a clearing
And advanced to the edge, keenly peering
Through the trees to see an astounding sight:
A stout man of more than usual height

With a flowing beard and dark, curly hair
Chanting while nodding his large head in prayer.
His words and manner to her appeared odd;
Apparently, he was addressing God.
Riding past the trees, she said, "Good morning."
He looked at them and without a warning,
Picked up a tall staff and prepared to fight.
"Kind sir, we mean no harm; do not take fright,
Nor find in us a cause for self-defense.
We intend only to inquire from whence

You come and what is, God's grace, that language?
Its meaning is more than I can manage."
"This tongue, dear lady, is known as Hebrew:
The proper language of prayer for a Jew.
Our rabbi claims it as ancient as Greek,
But I find it impossible to speak."
"Indeed," said William. "It is Greek to me;
And if impossible you need to see,
Why then I beg you try my native Welch,
That sounds to most ears like a donkey's belch."

"Enough, William, of this idle chatter;
I have need to ask some things that matter.
Pray tell, Excellency, what is a Jew?
I have once heard spoken of such as you
But only as concerns the lender's trade
That, to reverent Christians, God forbade."
"Ours, dear lady, is a tormented race
That endlessly wanders from place to place.
My religion, indeed, gave birth to yours;
We mourn Jerusalem that always lures.

My early years I spent in London town
With parents who revered the cap and gown
That scholars don. I prefer adventure,
A good fight and strong ale. Damn the censure
Of my pale and pusillanimous kin
Who have no fun - nor a pot to piss in.
As wandering tinker, I earn my keep;
Under the star-filled sky, I love to sleep.
But most of all, I crave venison stew:
I have been asked: 'Are you in truth a Jew?'

Meat tastes best when poached from a lord's preserve;
It's the least that we common folk deserve.
As an observant Jew, I say my prayers
Even making the rounds of the shire fairs.
I mend pots and pans and whatever else
The peasants have. I fix saddles and belts
And sharpen dull knives with a grinding stone
So that they cut right through gristle and bone."
Hearing this gave the maid a sudden start;
She felt a fleeting tremor in her heart.

"If dull knives thou canst so easily hone,
Canst thou temper swords on thy grinding stone?
If a fight thou love so well as you claim,
We have double reason to know your name
And seek to know if you will join our quest
For justice - but for now a place to rest
And there ponder how we three may proceed
To avenge a slaughter and by such deed
Bring blessed peace to England's war-torn shores.
We have had enough of ruinous wars."

"I like thy courageous words well enough –
Fashioned I would say out of sterner stuff
Than expected of one with soft tresses
More often found in rich, velvet dresses
Sitting in state at the banquet table

Or lying in bed with a French fable."
"Had you seen her slice off a foul rogue's ear
Or summon in these knaves a Godly fear,
Thou wouldst not take her bold words so lightly,"
Said William, his rude cheeks shining brightly.

"I stand here, my brave maiden, much abashed
At my intemperate words that have crashed
Like a ruffled partridge killed in mid-flight.   `
Jonah will be with you in your next fight."
"This Jonah," said Will, "would not suit a whale.
It must have been some silly, old wives' tale."
"Time," said the maiden, "to be on our way.
We must find a camp by the end of day."
"But let us keep the horse before the cart,"
Quoth Jonah. "Pray tell your name 'ere we start?"

William audaciously broke in anew:
"The Brave Maiden, methinks, fits like a shoe."
"Such antique sayings are the rage of late.
Though I hesitate to be tempting fate,
And while it might prove a prodigious load;
I'll gladly take the name thou hast bestowed
And hope, in God's name, to do it credit
While you, my new friends, will ne'er regret it.
But enough of this procrastination!
I fear we fail of our destination."

Touching a sharp spur to the chestnut's flank,
She approved the wisdom of her sly prank.
My true given name, I shall hide awhile -
Not through base cowardice, but rather guile.

IV

he Camp

The roseate sun was now far past noon;
They would surely need to be stopping soon.
The maiden rode at a vigorous pace,
Not letting the worry show in her face.
A sharp, gnawing chill suffused the bright air;
She yearned for a short rest but did not dare.
They had seen no safe places all day long
And might meet raw brigands in bands too strong
For the three of them to defeat alone.
She felt her spirits falling like a stone.

Luck had been with her for five days running:
More to do with luck, she thought, than cunning.
She had tried to maintain a watchful guard;
Staying alert had never been so hard.
She had needed to sleep from time to time:
Pure luck not to fall to a savage crime.
Traversing a somber wood, tall and dense,
She felt her weary nerves grow taut and tense.
A soft, soothing breeze touched her furrowed brow.
The breeze seemed to whisper: "Look around now."

She turned in time to see a smiling fox
Disappear through a thicket and loose rocks.
She tried hard to see where the fox had gone;
But though her search was diligent and long,
Of the fox, she saw neither hide nor hair.
It seemed to have vanished into thin air.
The thicket looked to be a solid mass
Of thorns and branches with no way to pass.
Just as she decided to ride on by,
A movement in the thicket caught her eye.

In the breeze, the branches began to sway;
To her surprise, she saw a passageway.
Motioning her companions to follow,
She proceeded slowly, her head bent low.
With caution, they advanced ten rods or more,
Hardly suspecting what fate had in store.
The passage was narrow, thorns caught their clothes.
About to turn back, they suddenly froze
And looked all around in shock and wonder.
The thicket was strangely torn asunder

Leaving them in a large, grassy clearing
Hidden from all human sight and hearing.
A crystal clear spring fed a bubbling stream;
She thought this must be a fantastic dream.
Slightly hidden behind a spindly fern,
She saw the elusive fox smile and turn
To trot off quickly through the waving ranks
Of ferns leaving no time to voice her thanks.
Not since she had in desperation fled
From the sight of friends and family dead,

Had she yet found a place to safely sleep
Without fear, and more, without cause to weep.
Overhanging rocks formed a shallow cave
That from the rude night wind some shelter gave
To the Brave Maiden and her band of two:
A yeoman's son and a wandering Jew.
She reflected sadly on this rough group.
How could she with such a powerless troop
Accomplish the bold plan she had in mind?
Somehow the wise Ormond she had to find.

And the march lords with their translucent pearls,
Will they be with her when her flag unfurls?
In her mind's eye, she saw a trampled field
And heard the clash of swords that angels wield.
Death's horses charged at furious paces,

Spurred by reapers with skeletal faces.
Death's vassals raced across a blood red sky;
Many a brave knight on this field would die.
She recoiled in mute horror from this day;
Something told her there was no other way.

Wrapped thus in thought as suppertime drew nigh,
Her gloomy vision caused a shallow sigh.
She barely saw Will standing at her feet.
"Milady, wouldst thou taste this roasted meat?"
"I see you have put your bow to good use
Whilst I have been dreaming with no excuse.
Tomorrow we put our camp in order
And make for ourselves a sturdy shelter.
I must also practice my archery
While you study infamous knavery."

Dark storm clouds rode the skies that chilly night;
Deep, rolling thunder gave Jonah a fright.
He awoke to watch the rain slanting down,
His brow deeply creased by a worried frown.
How came a hedonistic Jew like me
To follow this maiden's crusading plea.
In place of frothy ale and juicy boar,
I lie cold and drenched on this rocky floor.
I hesitate to think where she may lead;
The future holds many a daring deed.

Morning brought the sun in all its glory.
They set to work like the ancient story
Of the Pharaoh and the Israelite.
They worked from daybreak until evening's bright
Star brought their labors to a weary halt,
They ate a crude meal without herbs or salt.
"What I would give now," said the errant Jew,
"For some of that young widow's rabbit stew.
She herself looked like such a saucy dish;
Suited me just as well if she served fish."

Will ate his meal with a twinge of disgust.
"Regale us with brawling feats if you must,
But think of milady's delicate ears
When you long for widows of tender years."
"William, my thanks for your earnest concern;
But prithee, do you see my cheeks a burn?
Among fighting men, I spent goodly hours;
Their jokes would redden the palest flowers.
In the village, hard by our castle gate,
Nature's laws are learned with no prim debate.

Sheep and shaggy dogs have I seen mounted
So many times I have scarcely counted.
Farm life is not for the prating scholar,
Spouting speeches and wearing a collar.
Their tiresome lessons put me fast asleep
Without the age-old need for counting sheep.
To count the angels that fit on a pin
Is a task that I care not to begin.
Father sent for this dabbler from Bedford;
His pedantry left me completely bored.

He walked on muddy paths with lifted hem;
He noisily cleared his dry throat of phlegm.
Outdoors, he was wont to expectorate.
His love of fowl we could not satiate.
He finally was his own undoing:
Caught half naked in the village wooing.
In a rage, Father had him soundly whipped
And back to Bedford, he was promptly shipped.
I confess I did not mourn his parting
Nor yearn for his spitting and loud farting.

Now, my dear William, dost thou plainly see:
The facts of nature are not new to me?"
Over William's broad face spread disbelief,
From which he sought to gain some quick relief.
"But then, milady, how came you to read?

In what manner was planted learning's seed?"
"My Mother was a lady much refined
(And here another thought lay just behind);
With her, formal lessons were much more fun.
Music, French, and the movement of the sun

Around the earth were daily, bookish tasks
That she enlivened by most cheerful masques
In which soldiers and servants had a part.
Father, the villain, was thrust through the heart.
Always were the village folk invited;
The small children were the most delighted.
The castle rang with loud peals of laughter:
Fond memories to carry hereafter.
But now, my kind friends let us take our rest
And in safety sleep in our new-built nest."

Speaking thus, the Maiden ruffled her hair
And took a deep breath of the crisp, night air.
Cruel and difficult times lay ahead,
But sufficient for now to go to bed.
In the bright morning, fresh ideas would grow;
And she would conquer that tautly strung bow.
She heard in the distance a lone wolf howl
And much closer in, the screech of an owl.
Again, the soft breeze whispered in her ear:
Indistinct phrases that were far from clear.

Not knowing exactly the reason why,
She fell soundly asleep and did not cry.

V

he Twins

Of supple saplings, they had built a hut;
And this morning, she planned to figure what
Was needed to shelter the chestnut mare.
Animals she felt needed special care:
A thought oft unknown in that cruel age,
But one taught her by that most worthy sage,
Ormond, loyal teacher and trusted guide
Who often went on her fast morning ride.
He spoke of life's magic and mystery,
Of England's long and tragic history.

He always carried a fine, tempered sword
Though he was neither baron nor rich lord.
He could employ his sword to great effect;
But for books and laws, he had more respect.
He taught her to distinguish right from wrong.
Solace he found in the nightingale's song.
He warned her of England's perilous state
And the need somehow to escape this fate.
Grievously missing him as she wandered;
Has he met his death, she sadly pondered.

Jonah lost his smile when he heard the news;
 For a moment, she thought he might refuse.
"Brave Maiden, we worked all day yesterday;
I had other plans in mind if I may.
The nearest village would suit rather well;
We shall return before the evening bell."
Added William, "I'll bring down a swift hind;
We've had no venison, need I remind."
She addressed them in a tone, grave and stern
Such as gave them each quite a nasty turn.
"Tomorrow shall we explore our domain,

But not while more important tasks remain."
Chastened, they set to work on a shelter
Though their work was rather helter skelter.
They wove a rustic roof of tender boughs.
"Good enough," said Jonah, "For sheep or cows."
The roof was tightly fixed to solid trees,
The sides left open to the sylvan breeze.
Flame made no apparent complaint at all -
Though no resemblance to her castle stall.

Beneath her lean belly, Flame tucked her legs.
Building shelters, she thought, is fine but begs
The question of killing the evil count.
For that, we'll need much more than just one mount.
The Maiden was hard at target practice -
Relentless as in her thirst for justice.
She fitted an arrow to her drawn bow
And felt surging strength through her fingers flow.
Swift flew the arrow, but a hair breadth's wide,
Nicking towering Jonah in the side.

"Dear God in Heaven, now what have I done?
After a day's work in the glaring sun?"
"Fair shot, milady," shouted Will with glee.
"I would surely not be thine enemy."
"Oh dear," she said in a voice less than curt.
"I fervently pray that you are not hurt."
"Fear not, Brave Maiden. Nothing but a scratch.
'Twill heal nicely with a simple cloth patch.
And Will, shed none of your crocodile tears;
To feast and brawl, I have many more years.

But I beg, Brave Maiden, for our own good
Practice a tad 'ere meeting Robin Hood."
"Now dost thou believe that old legend true?
Perhaps you believe in King Arthur too.
No shining Galahad will join our cause
To give England lasting peace and just laws.

Sustenance will come only from ourselves:
Neither from misty ghosts nor forest elves."
"But," cried William hoarsely, "We are but three."
"Not for long, friend William, as you shall see."

Next morning at sunup, they left the camp
With the grass still wet and their clothing damp.
Passing the thicket, she saw a bright flash
Of red as the smiling fox made a dash
For the woods, pausing just to wink at her.
It had luminous eyes and gleaming fur.
"Please wait," she called. "What does this really mean?
Are you something other than you would seem?"
The answer, sadly, she had sought in vain;
The wily fox ran down the wooded lane.

They heard just then furious shouts - and words
That stirred up flocks of angry, screeching birds.
Searching to see who would such turmoil raise,
They found a frantic scene that did amaze:
Two men with looks and dress identical
Hurling barbs in a way most comical.
"What sayest thou? Why you shall rue the day?"
"Christ and God's blood, now I shall make thee pay."
Seething with rage, they hefted wooden swords.
From each of their belts hung several gourds.

They each fought with truly consummate skill,
Cursing wildly as if ready to kill.
The fight was equal, and neither could win -
Nor commit that savage, Biblical sin.
The forest rang with tempestuous blows;
But at her commanding voice, both men froze.
They looked slowly around in shocked surprise
To see a maiden with fire in her eyes.
But what gave one a more violent start
Was the sharp arrow leveled at his heart.
"What misery, brother against brother -

Better far, the love they owe each other!
I bemoan these harsh times that are awry:
To witness such scenes and not wonder why."
"Milady, we simply love to duel;
Our bloody threats are but to play the fool."
"What brings two yeomen then so far a field?
Have you no budding crops whose fruited yield
Depends largely on your sweat-drenched labor
And whose wholesome bread you hope to savor?"

"We have of late from our homes been driven
And from our kinsmen cruelly riven.
Having twice been ravaged by Count Gerard,
Our scared villagers thought their fortunes marred.
Twins, like witches, they said, bring evil luck;
Grain withers on the stalk, and calves don't suck
Their mothers' milk." "The opposite I've heard,"
The Maiden said. "And find both views absurd.
Come proud twins; join us for a hearty meal.
Perhaps we can soon find you swords of steel."

VI

 Fire

Joy-provoking Spring now burst all her bounds;
The forest overflowed with cheerful sounds.
Birds of varied stripe and hue roamed the sky
As anxious mothers taught their young to fly.
Newly horned bucks sprang over fallen logs;
Razor-tusked boars rooted in mossy bogs.
Foxes and wolves were on a deadly prowl,
Teaching young hunters with a muted growl.
Woodpeckers feasted on beetles and grubs;
Mother bears watched over rough-tumbling cubs.

The Maiden rode forth with her band of five;
Rarely had they felt more fully alive.
In the camp, they had continued to build;
Betimes, they joked, they would elect a guild.
They moved at a brisk pace, senses alert
For dangers to face, or perhaps, to skirt.
Each carried a bow slung across the back,
A score of arrows in a deerskin pack.
She rode in front, her reddish hair flowing,
Her head held high, her ruddy cheeks glowing.

Flame alone felt high-strung and oddly tense;
Trouble was brewing said her mare's sixth sense.
The mare snorted and shook her tangled mane;
The Maiden gently slackened her tight rein.
Selwyn, one brother, was cursing the pox
When the Maiden happened to see the fox.
Before she had time to react or speak,
The other twin sprang ahead like a streak;
And pointing to smoke darkening the sky,
Thin Egbert let out an ear-splitting cry.
Across a small meadow dotted with sheep,

Far removed from manor or castle keep,
Stood a lonely, impoverished village
Which four vicious knights had come to pillage.
Spotting Gerard's coat of arms on a shield,
The Maiden spurred the mare across the field.
Bleating in fear, the sheep scattered and fled;
She let go the reins and gave Flame her head.
Arriving as a knight wrestled a goat,
She shot a barbed arrow straight through his throat.

"Practice makes perfect," said Jonah with glee,
Crippling a knight with a blow to the knee.
A third was tying grain sacks on his horse;
Selwyn and Egbert stopped him in mid-course.
As he reached to unsheathe his sword in vain,
They twisted his arms in hot, searing pain.
The fourth knight was beating a bent old man;
Flame managed to kick him right in the can.
Releasing the knights *sans* weapons or steeds,
She advised them to forego evil deeds.

"Tell your master that before very long,
His cunning head will not be worth a song.
Justice, order and peace shall England see,
I swear by God for all eternity."
"Who are you?" inquired a knight in dismay.
"The Brave Maiden gave thee justice this day,"
Replied William in stentorian tones.
"Now remove your friend and bury his bones."
The spreading fire took all morning to quench;
They held their noses from the smoke and stench

Of charred goose feathers and smoldering thatch.
"How," she asked, "Did your forlorn village catch
The attention of Gerard's brutal fiends.
To speak the truth, you have barely the means
To sustain yourselves." "Our unpaid taxes
Brought them here with swords and battle axes."

"You shall have my protection! Now farewell."
I wonder, thought Flame, how in holy hell,
She will make that outrageous promise stick.
Is anyone else not completely thick?

They rode calmly, four horses to the good,
Laughing and rejoicing, as well they should.
The twins, suitably armed with well-honed swords,
Were eager to fight any heathen hordes.
As the bright afternoon began to wane,
A spunky village lad caught them and fain
Would add his strong arm to their noble band.
Smiling, she extended a welcome hand.

VII

Recruits

As dramatic tales of their exploits spread,
And highwaymen began to live in dread;
Her audacious band saw its fortunes grow,
Proving anew that ye reap as ye sow.
Two infamous robbers caught in the act,
With the flats of broadswords were soundly whacked.
With this wise sentence, they were so impressed
That they pleaded to join - who could have guessed.
A scoundrel, though, who murdered for a fee;
She hung by the neck from a live oak tree.

Merchants he had terrorized for ages -
Leaving a trail of blood and outrages.
Long a vassal of Philip the Cruel
(Whose domains lived under barbarous rule),
He earned from his master a rich tribute
By killing those who would not contribute
What Phillip demanded for protection.
Those few that ignored the implication
Paid a price that was exceedingly high:
Widows and orphans left to mourn and cry.

Thus, a double profit was provided:
Gold for his coffers, subjects divided
By anguish and shame and so twice oppressed.
Against both body and soul, he transgressed.
Thinking only of gold, banquets and hawks;
Philip held to the rule that money talks.
Daily feasting on sumptuous repasts,
His love of cruelty went unsurpassed.
Copious wine gave him a bulbous nose;
He was schooled in neither rich verse nor prose.

Cringing servants quaked if he looked askance;
To do someone ill, he ne'er missed a chance.
His vast belly round as a washing tub;
He had his pate, with oil, a servant rub.
In short, he was not a good man to mock;
He would rob a man down to the last frock.
The murderer was caught in a tavern
On the high road near the town of Malvern.
Witnesses and jury were common folk;
Pronouncing sentence, with fierce pride she spoke.

Daring women and men flocked to her side
As such bold deeds became known far and wide.
They came from all regions and walks of life,
Hoping to end England's blood-thirsty strife:
Desperate peasants deprived of their land
By corrupt earls who with steel-fisted hand
Evicted serfs who had long paid their dues
In favor of those with nothing to lose
By offering to pay a few pence more
To harrow the fields and sleep on the floor;

An apprentice sick of his leather guild -
Full of importance and rather self-willed
Whose harsh master beat him once too often,
Fleeing in rage from what seemed a coffin;
A youthful cobbler with his fill of shoes -
So wretched that boredom caused him to choose
To leave his dreary bench and tools behind
And seek what high adventures he could find.
Some came with motives pure and others mixed,
But each of them knew something must be fixed.

Annabelle was a painter of renown;
Her pictures commanded more than a crown.
One day as she put the final touches
On a portrait of a haughty Duchess,
She heard the Duke boast to a meek vassal:

"Their heads will top the walls of a castle,
And that will teach this Maiden to meddle
And impertinent justice to peddle."
Annabelle, with a gasp, set down her brush
And left, without thought, the room in a rush:

Pausing only to spit on the portrait
Though her fee, and head, would now go forfeit.
She had heard, of late, the common folk talk
Of a Brave Maiden who had yet to balk
At using her potent sword or longbow
To protect the weak or oppose a foe.
Annabelle proudly came from humble stock;
Her father, a freeman, kept a small flock
Of sheep and nimble goats for wool and meat.
At the market, her mother took a seat

And sold whatever their holdings produced:
Her profits handsome though greatly reduced
By taxes and the High Sheriff's demands.
The country abounded with greedy hands
To steal the ripened fruits of honest toil -
Earned by rank sweat from the richly dark soil.
By her mother's stool, she began to draw:
Her portraits limned always without a flaw.
She astounded the townsfolk one and all
Who took to standing near the market stall.

Her talent would have surely gone to waste
But for a wise woman with wealth and taste
Who saw a drawing of her kitchen maid
And provided lessons - expenses paid.
Annabelle studied from dawn until dusk;
The master's manner was quiet but brusque.
Annabelle acquired the painter's technique:
How to flatter and turn fat into sleek.
To wealthy merchants, she charged a fat fee;
Her poor peasant friends, she painted for free.

She galloped away with her eyes ablaze -
Emotions whirling, her mind in a daze.
How to find the Maiden she had no clue;
But, without pausing, she knew what to do.
She rode through fields and along muddy tracks
And slept on the floors of cold, peasant shacks.
She told her hosts the news that she carried,
And they all said wise not to have tarried.
Alongside the paths, serfs pointed the way,
Calling God bless and bowing heads to pray

That the Maiden she would reach with good speed;
Whose life might now hang by a slender reed.
Nearing the immense forest of Blaxford;
Of the Maiden, none had recently heard
Or knew how to find her wide-roaming band.
Annabelle feared they had fled this fair land
Of forested hills and broad, green meadows
Dotted with fat sheep and lined with hedgerows
Whose ripe buds now shone in all their glory.
What if swift time had stolen her story?

Thinking perhaps that she was not trusted,
She found an inn with its doorknob rusted.
The air was thick, the ceiling black from smoke.
A rough-clad barmaid went over to poke
The embers into flames, her greasy cap
Askew. One eye socket veiled by a flap
Of skin caused Annabelle to start in fear.
"Why, whatever could be the matter, dear?
Have you never seen such a rare beauty?"
Agreeing from her keen sense of duty,

Annabelle inquired of the Maiden's camp.
"Who wants to know: a nonsensical tramp
Of a girl seeking adventure and fun,
Who, at the first clash of steel, will then run
To hide her ostrich-like head in the sand?

Now wouldn't that sight be awfully grand?"
Annabelle wept, swore an oath, and pleaded
Until convinced, the one-eyed maid ceded
And told of a path with nary a trace.
"How will I be sure when I reach the place?"

The barmaid smirked: "The camp is well-hidden.
No one enters there who is not bidden."
Annabelle nodded and started to leave
When an evil-smelling drunk grabbed her sleeve.
"Come grace my lap; now there's a pretty lass."
She cried out in horror: "Please let me pass."
The barmaid roughly knocked him to the floor
And, winking, led Annabelle out the door.
Annabelle rode for two days and a night,
Until halted by an amazing sight.

Almost hidden behind a pile of rocks,
Annabelle swore she saw a smiling fox.

VIII

arah

Though heartily welcomed into the fold,
Annabelle's news left the Maiden's eyes cold.
"We have now a cause - justice - that we serve;
And from this mission, we shall never swerve
Until peace reigns once more in this rich land.
It is on this ground that we make our stand:
The peasant unafraid shall tend his farm;
The saintly pilgrim travel free from harm;
The merchant fairly taxed pursue his trade;
The market woman in true coin be paid.

Only blind has justice any true worth,
Favoring neither high nor humble birth.
Princesses and dukes must merit respect;
Their duty, at their peril, they neglect.
With nobility comes obligation;
To serve is the noblest occupation.
Sound laws, by the King, must be well enforced;
And they must, by the barons, be endorsed.
The King shall abandon his greedy ways,
Or see counted the number of his days.

Your worrisome report leaves me unfazed;
Were the Duke other, I would be amazed.
Consider perhaps to best use your time
Not gilding a painting, but fighting crime."
"I would fain, Brave Maiden, lay down my paints
To acquire the hard skill of thrusts and feints.
But could not this artist in truth surmise;
To both paint and fight would be worldly wise?
And if I could please be so bold to ask
If to common folk you assign a task

In this government of justice and law?
If not, therein lies a most fatal flaw."
"Indeed, commoners must play their own part;
Or even good laws, they take not to heart.
I know not how this can be quickly done;
First, crimson battles must be fought and won.
On the morrow, you begin your training;
We would start now, but the day is waning.
We train daily with longbow, sword and lance;
Thus, we leave nothing to pitiless chance.

We study tactics and war's history.
We have as well a fledgling armory
Where our weapons we fashion and refine.
With arms, yon Jonah is like a gold mine.
Now, gold coin is something we sorely lack;
Without which, we take a different tack.
We have long lists of goods we need to buy;
Countless provisions are in short supply.
We need ground wheat and rye to bake our bread;
We eat roast game and bake wild grains instead.

For shields and armor, we lack plates of steel;
Sometimes it all makes my head spin and reel.
To sew new outfits, we need bolts of cloth;
To think, but not to act, would make me wroth.
I know impatience is a deadly sin;
But at times, I wonder where to begin.
The cobbler is working a damaged hide;
Good Jonah assures me God will provide.
But you have journeyed very long and hard;
So, this conversation, we shall retard

Until you have eaten and rested well.
I shall talk with thee at the morning bell."

The camp rose with the dawn and set to work;
There were none who even wanted to shirk.
Cheerfully, they greeted one another.
For victory, they must help each other.
Will, the yeoman's son, taught the archer's skill,
The quarreling twins how with swords to kill.
Mock wooden knights were used as practice foes
That splintered and fell under savage blows.
Jonah sweated at a hot, rustic forge;
On succulent game, he still yearned to gorge.

The Maiden that morning, rode out alone.
To melancholy, she was rarely prone;
But today she had need of solitude
To think clearly and plan with fortitude.
Resting on a rock by a quiet stream,
She mused while watching a silvery bream.
She smelt in the air wild, tangy onions
And longed for more than loyal companions.
Gentle Will, she knew, loved her with passion;
In turn, she could but offer compassion.

Just then, she felt a breeze mussing her hair
And a cold presence disturbing the air.
She looked around and saw before her eyes
A vicious, snarling wolf - monstrous in size.
Flame, with her sword fastened to the saddle,
Had strayed. No sword would fight in this battle.
From her belt hung the dagger with the crest:
Not nearly enough, even at her best.

The huge wolf growled fiercely and bared its teeth.
The Maiden trembled like an autumn leaf,

But a dim memory rose in her mind.
She reached into her leather pouch to find
The mysterious coin of strange design.
She held it high up so the light could shine
On its mystic symbols and worn surface.
The wolf, in an instant, changed its purpose
And crawled towards her with an abject mien -
A more astounding sight she had ne'er seen.
The tamed wolf licked her hand and laid its head
Across her lap while she caressed the dread

Creature between the ears. As in a trance,
She spoke softly – struck by this happenstance.
"This is a phenomenon passing strange:
To see a fearsome brute so quickly change
Into a fawning creature mild and meek.
I would we had a common tongue to speak.
I know not what power brought you to me;
But from now on, Sarah, your name shall be.
At this moment, the grazing mare appeared;
And sensing the wolf, on her hind legs reared.

"Fear not, Flame, we have found a welcome friend;
So, calm yourself and let us homeward wend."
A hungry wolf, thought Flame: a friend indeed!
Those razor teeth are what we really need!

IX

 Troublesome Knight

Spirits high, she rode joyfully for home;
Sarah took to the fragrant woods to roam.
Slender blue bells had sprouted everywhere
While sweet honeysuckle perfumed the air.
Summer reigned in each clearing and bower
Where drone bees dashed from flower to flower.
Honey, she thought, would be a handsome treat
And make withal a slice of bread complete.
So thinking, she uttered a troubled sigh;
We'll certainly procure gold by and by.

Passing through the forest from north to south,
The highroad ended at a river mouth.
This well-worn thoroughfare lay near her way.
Outlaws abounded with old debts to pay
(Including one whose thumb was newly gone -
Caught red-handed by the Maiden at dawn
Stealing a family's last bag of grain.
Lucky indeed for him he was not slain.)
And hoping to profit from misfortune.
She drew nigh this wide road with due caution.

From the road arose a fearsome medley
Of sounds: a fight that looked to be deadly.
She saw a young knight with thick, tousled hair
Hurling outrageous taunts into the air
And wielding his sword with broad, sweeping arcs
Against six men who bore the bloody marks
Of fierce combat on every cloak and limb.
Yet the prospects of his winning seemed slim.
The six men rode laden with bulging sacks
Fixed snugly with straps on their chargers' backs.

The Maiden galloped right into the fray,
Never one to let odds get in her way.
Thrusting with her sword, she unhorsed a foe.
The knight laughed, "How a merry wind doth blow
'Twixt that varlet's ass and his saddle seat."
He landed a charging knight at his feet.
The woods rang with the din of steel on steel;
For quarter, there was no point to appeal.
The knight suffered a slight gash on one arm;
The Maiden's face showed excessive alarm.

"Fear not, 'tis but a harmless, piddling wound;
But lay on hard, fair maid, or we are doomed.
And pray, what makes a gentle maid so bold;
Are you after Gerard's ill-gotten gold?"
The Maiden stayed her hand in complete shock.
"Beleaguered knight, dost thou so often mock?
I joined this hot fight with but one concern;
Six against one is hardly a fair turn."
These words did not cause her bright, blushing cheek;
Of other thoughts, she did not choose to speak.

Instinct made her wheel in time to parry
And lunge forward hard enough to carry
Her terrified opponent from the field.
Her powerful strike cut in half his shield.
"In that case, once these fetid villains flee,
Take the honor; and leave the gold to me."
"But gold," she cried, "Will satisfy our needs.
And justice requires more than noble deeds."
Two Gerard lackeys now each aimed a lance
At the Maiden who hardly stood a chance

'Til her assailants froze dead in their tracks,
And the hair stood straight up on their scarred backs
At a sight neither really cared to see
And that just about caused them both to pee.
Sarah emitted a deep, frightening growl

And bared her fangs in a furious scowl.
She was the biggest wolf they could conceive;
They moved not a step and could scarcely breathe.
Sarah leapt, and a fulsome spurt of blood
Poured forth from a knave in a scarlet flood

As she spliced an artery in his neck.
He fell dead to the ground, a twitching wreck.
His comrade ran howling in mad disgrace,
A mark of horror engraved on his face.
The final two varlets in terror fled,
Leaving on the wooded road, three knaves dead.
As the weary knight fought to stem his fears,
The Maiden scratched Sarah between her ears.
"Is this a wolf, a dog or a demon?
The latter, I would think, to see them run."

"Nothing more than a common wolf is she,
But one who seems exceeding fond of me."
She grinned and gently rubbed the antique coin.
The knight buckled his sword around his groin.
"Against great odds, thou hast seen some service;
Wilt thou as well serve the cause of justice?"
She felt, with this question, her heart compress;
And feelings stir that she would not confess.
Suppressing these thoughts, she surveyed the scene,
Then turned to face him with a sterner mien.

"I thank thee kindly – a worthy offer;
But I would prefer to fill my coffer
With the fruits of Gerard's ill-gotten gains,
For which, we have gone to substantial pains."
"Hast not a knight some more noble design
Than stealing gold no matter how condign
The loss to that most foul, barbarous earl?
Sir, play not the part of a low-born churl."
"Now, my maid, wherein lies the difference?
Because you claim your theft in reverence

To the glory of some higher calling?
Rotten curs there are aplenty, bawling
Out their bulging eyes in a fiery Hell
Who, on any Sunday, your tale would tell.
I, myself, was raised as an honest knight,
Amidst gracious acres – a most welcome sight.
God had blessed our smiling, fertile treasure
With sunshine and rain in equal measure.
Our granaries were plentifully stuffed,
The peasants' cheeks and bellies nicely puffed.

The village held a merry springtide dance,
And love caught fire with a mere passing glance.
Storehouses are now bare, cornstalks blighted;
The people's lives barren and benighted;
And hunger rules supreme where laughter reigned.
To serve your great cause would for me seem feigned.
The seeds of despair, Count Gerard has sown;
With this gold, I recover but our own.
Yet, thou art a brave, impetuous lass.
I would not leave thee with an empty glass

(Nor forswear the considerable help
Of your sword arm and that over-sized whelp)
So in equal parts, we shall share the gold
And in fond remembrance, this day shall hold."
The Maiden's eyes now shone with a new light:
"Thy sorrowful tale makes me feel contrite
And reminds me of others that I know.
What you propose is fair, so let us go
Our separate ways and in God's own time,
May our kingdom at last be free of crime.

Of today's work, I have but one remorse:
Three slain men who only served a vile, coarse
Master and so did not deserve to die."
"Over such knaves, you have no need to cry.
Their sharp falchions they put to wicked use,

And they were widely known for their abuse
Of the wise, antique customs of our shire.
Yet I will build them a funeral pyre;
Or rather, see to it that graves be dug,
Then toast their going with a brimming mug."

Homeward the Maiden rode sadly oppressed
Despite with gold and two new horses blessed.
Heavy were her thoughts and not less her heart;
From that tousled knight, she was loath to part.
The big wolf gamboled cheerfully behind,
And the dark cloud soon lifted from her mind.
She tingled with glee at the camp's surprise:
To return with a wolf and golden prize,
Having left for a simple morning ride
And now richly dowered like an earl's bride!

X

The French Student

Verdant summer, in slow steps, turned to fall.
Will patiently followed the wild duck's call
And brought to camp many a tasty dish;
Venison was still Jonah's fervent wish.
Nights were chilly as the days grew shorter.
Around the bright fires, a pint of porter
Accompanied ancient tales and good cheer.
The Maiden allowed each a mug of beer.
With Jonah and Annabelle, she - for hours -
Spoke of strategies and the due powers

That adhere to king or nobility.
That a balance was needed she could see.
But how, wisely, to make it come to pass?
And what role for the growing merchant class?
With the gold, they were now well-provisioned
To fight the hard war she had envisioned
Would bring her sacred quest to victory.
Though in her ranks were knights of chivalry;
Of tough, seasoned fighters, she had but few.
And something else, she felt, was missing too.

As reports of her cause had grown and spread,
And rumor upon truth had amply fed,
Ardent men and women of every stripe
Were drawn to her as to Saint Patrick's pipe.
She promised them neither profit nor loss
But asked each to swear by the Holy Cross
To fight for justice, order and reform
And hold to the course no matter the storm.
The camp sounded like a festive beehive;
What a glorious time to be alive!

The twins one day went for a woodland walk,
Seeking, no doubt, a quiet place to talk
About their practice with the battle axe.
"Let's see how our Sir Percival reacts
When we display for him our new routine.
'Twill be the best by far he's ever seen."
Percival was a well-reputed knight;
The twins had despised this oaf at first sight.
He had recently joined her retinue
And often told the Maiden what to do.

Self-important in martial history,
He held forth at length on its mystery
With frequent tales of the war-like Roman.
He told her how best to site her bowmen.
On the use of horse, he explicated.
His sanguine exploits, he replicated.
He had won every battle of the age.
His feats of arms were difficult to gauge.
He told Jonah how armor should be made;
His lustrous fame would clearly never fade.

He was quite a tall and gangly fellow,
With a pimply nose and cheeks of yellow.
He belched and snored out loud at every mass;
The twins took him for an egregious ass.
The Maiden heard his remarks politely,
Then his wise counsel ignored forthrightly.
Jonah nodded as if deep in some prayer,
Then responded with a serious air:
"A most excellent point: if pigs could fly;
I wager thou wouldst make a fine rabbi."

Recalling this, Selwyn rocked with laughter.
"May Sir P soon pee in the hereafter.
At the word, 'rabbi', didst thou see his face?
Sir P a Jew? Dear God, what a disgrace!"
Giggling, Egbert fell in a pile of leaves.

"For fun though, nothing beats those greedy reeves
Who complain and holler at being fleeced.
They are merely from guilt being released!
Their money goes to feed the luckless poor -
And to buy scarce provisions, to be sure."

Annabelle is charged with buying supplies.
In the market, she must watch out for spies
Since Gerard seeks the camp - so far in vain.
No serf will tell despite the cruel pain
That Gerard's vicious knights love to inflict.
The time approaches for mortal conflict.
The Maiden trains hard her growing forces -
Both on foot and mounted on their horses.
Her men and women are in fighting trim
And plan to hang Gerard from a high limb.

The twins soon found a secluded meadow
And rested by an overgrown barrow,
The grave of a hero from ancient times -
Gone ere his brave tale could be writ in rhymes.
Talking in the noonday sun, sleep, like death,
Arrived unannounced. Just a supple breath
Escaped their parted lips while inside boiled
Unforeseen passions - untamed and unspoiled
That might explode someday in vengeful rage
To alter the course of this anguished age.

So securely did sleep now enfold them
That had a grinning sprite whispered: "Ahem"
For sleeping when the whole world was teeming,
That merry fay would have found them dreaming -
Undisturbed by a cheerful, manly voice
Singing as if the forest should rejoice
At serenading in such fine fashion -
And rendered with so much verve and passion
That his chorale he thought a gracious boon.
Too bad he was completely out of tune.

The songbirds ceased their chattering chorus
And listened as if to lines from Horace.
Two cavorting swallows paused in mid-flight;
Two hares and a wry mole ducked out of sight.
A fey roebuck and doe stared in wonder,
As if rapt by distant peals of thunder.
Were his plainsong not enough to bemuse,
Add to it his habit of brilliant hues.
His coat was dazzling in its varied sheen.
His leggings were of scarlet and dark green -

In colors alternating for both legs.
From his pommel hung a basket of eggs.
He held his seat with a high-born swagger;
He wore, in his belt, a crested dagger.
His singing, at long last, the twins awoke.
They thought at first it must be a bad joke:
A wraith braying in a concocted tongue.
They then were sure the Doomsday bell had rung.
"What fiend is making this caterwauling?"
 "Only a madman could cause such bawling!"

The singer rode into the verdant field,
And, noticing the twins, to them appealed:
"Pardonnez-moi, je suis un peu perdu."
Their eyes bulged as if they had seen a gnu:
"Art thou a man or some magical beast?
Thy clothes to our eyes are a wondrous feast,
But thy words most preposterous and weird.
Thou cast on us a curse, we are afeard."
"Ah, *mais certainment*, you must me excuse;
It was neither a curse nor wicked ruse.

I sometimes forget to speak in *anglais*;
I am French and was thus speaking *francais*."
"While," said Egbert, "He now speaks normally,
His apparel is an anomaly."
"Where," asked Selwyn, "Did you learn that odd word?"

"At supper ... the Maiden ... I overheard ..."
"The Maiden," broke in the Frenchman with glee.
"It is she whom I came from France to see.
In this dense forest, I had lost my way.
If thou leads me to her, I will thee pay."

These welcome words got their full attention,
And they both concurred without abstention
To serve as guides for this peacock from France.
Their meager fee they asked for in advance.
"But tell us, dear friend, how we may thee call."
"In French, my proper name is Pierre of Gaul."
"Why then follow us, our good pee in air.
If thou canst learn to fight near half as fair
As hast conquered French with proper accent,
Our time and thy money are aptly spent."

The Maiden gaped at this startling vision.
Annabelle shook her head in derision.
Jonah chortled and tugged at his full beard
While several of the lads smirked and jeered.
Fashion in camp ran to dull, somber shades;
Such eye-popping splendor was for coy maids.
The women fighters all dressed simply too.
The Maiden had warned the band to eschew
The multi-hued plumage to which aspired
Parvenu earls and was at court required.

A hard-muscled young lad stood in Pierre's way
And inquired if the clown would care to play
At swords. Perhaps dancing were more his style.
The callow youth then flashed an evil smile,
And two other lads begged to have a go.
Pierre quite calmly said that he hoped to show
Such courtesy as he was always taught
That he even owed to scum. Now he sought
To chide them, not singly, but together
Since their swords would sting much like a feather.

Three mortal blades flashed in the autumn sun,
But Pierre laughed as if it were just good fun.
The forest resounded with clashing steel
And brutish grunts that made one's blood congeal.
Sword whirling as if of its own accord,
Pierre acted as if he were slightly bored
As he pinned one fellow against a tree
And calmly felled another with his knee.
With the third, he traded bone-crushing blows;
The cheering audience was on their toes.

The Maiden was suddenly heard to shout:
"Stop right now: enough of this foolish bout.
Fighting we shall have in great abundance.
This is a command I shall give but once."
The two fighters froze their swords in mid-stroke,
Like schoolboys caught in a practical joke.
Eyeing each other in wary silence,
They knew not how to end the violence
When Mathew grasped Pierre with both bearish paws.
"My skilled friend!" he exclaimed. "We all have flaws.

I am known for a too ready temper -
Always ready to holler '*sic semper*'.
You, in contrast, have a clear, steady mind
But must, perforce, be wholly color blind."
The four combatants then hugged each other,
And Pierre was proclaimed as a true brother
Who needed only a new set of clothes.
Like the phoenix, a brand-new man arose.
He greeted the Maiden, bowing with grace.
A look of surprise spread across her face.

"The crested dagger that you boldly wear -
So like mine own that they make a fine pair.
Came it in your possession honestly -
And I charge thee answer right modestly;
Or didst thou obtain it through thievery

Or some other form of skullduggery?"
"Why dear cousin - for that is what we are -
How could you, in good conscience, freely mar
My reputation and your own good name:
Your own – and mine - since they are both the same!

Some distant relations you have in France,
Who receiving news of your gallant stance -
And too of the vile, murderous events
That cost you a brother and both parents -
Have hastened me to give service and aid
And further your quest with a tempered blade."
"Your kind assistance, I shall not refuse;
But how, dear Cousin, did you hear the news?"
"Your worthy father had a faithful friend
Who has crossed to France for this very end.

A substantial force he intends to raise
And plans to set sail within thirty days.
But my country has troubles of her own;
The land is rent by war, the people groan."
"I would fain hear the name of whom you speak.
If Ormond, he fares like the antique Greek
And overcomes grave trials and dangers
To garner help among far off strangers."
"Ormond was indeed the proud name he gave.
Hearing him discourse made my sword a slave

Of thy great cause and too bloody labor.
I cajoled from my father this favor,
So he with mixed pride and pain did agree
To my fronting the grave and stormy sea."
"Ormond alive and shortly on his way;
For greater bliss, I would not dare to pray."
The Maiden clapped her graceful hands with joy.
Then Annabelle spoke looking shy and coy:
"Those large, brown eggs, kind sir, look freshly laid;
We'll give whatever you deem fair in trade."

Pierre briefly glanced her way and in a thrice,
Lost his heart for a seeming modest price.
Her dark eyes were pools of infinite space.
She had cherry lips in an oval face
With sleek, raven hair that composed a frame.
Her cheeks could put the fairest rose to shame.
"What kind trade dost thou offer?" Pierre stuttered.
"Oh dear: first love," Jonah softly muttered.
"A roast goose," she said. "With a crackling skin;
A rich, dark sauce to dip a biscuit in;

Mincemeat and apple pies; a tangy cheese;
A hearty wine you can drink to the lees;
And with those eggs, a frothy omelet
To finish a feast you'll not soon forget."
An innocent strand fell across one eye;
Her piercing glance was guileless - and yet sly.
Cheeks afire, bold Pierre mutely bowed his head
While the Maiden kindly spoke in his stead:
"My cousin's journey has indeed been long;
Let us show our welcome with food and song.

Tonight, we have good reason to rejoice.
Great France will raise her formidable voice
And will give succor to our noble cause.
Soon enough will we pull John's vicious claws."
As usual, thought Flame, a bit naïve;
In France, I'm not so ready to believe.

XI

he Raid

The camp was in a furious bustle
Preparing for a vigorous tussle.
A scared serf had arrived in camp at dusk;
He spoke coarsely, and his manner was brusque.
His long hair was matted, his clothing dank;
And he told a tale that of evil stank.
His village lay within Philip's domain,
Who imposed a harsh rule with might and main.
His sobriquet he earned with room to spare;
There was no cruelty he did not dare.

In the village lived a happy couple.
A dark beauty, she was slim and supple.
They spent their days growing barley and rye.
Philip saw her one day while riding by.
Her beauty struck a hot spark of desire.
That same day his fat reeve came to require
The maid's presence at the castle forthwith.
What next occurred has the air of a myth.
The faithful beauty refused to comply.
Her stout husband gave the reeve a black eye,

Who ran for his horse wailing and cursing.
His bloody nose would likewise need nursing.
Hearing the news, Philip was mortified;
His sharp lust, with rage, was now fortified.
Next morning, in the rain, to their hovel,
Philip sent four knights to make them grovel.
The couple stood tall refusing to bend.
Threatened by the knights with a gruesome end,
They were flailed with swords and dragged through the mud.
Their faces torn and encrusted with crud,

They were thrown in a cart and hauled to jail,
Leaving three young children to weep and wail.
They lay on the floor of an unlit cell.
"Tomorrow I shall send them both to Hell,"
Laughed Philip gaily as he slapped his knee.
"Beheading is such a fine sight to see.
A good lesson to teach this scum their place,
Mercy will have no cause to show her face."
Heralds rode forth the event to proclaim;
Philip felt not an iota of shame.

The serf finished his strange tale of sorrow:
"But for you, my sister dies tomorrow."
The Maiden felt uncontrolled anger surge.
Such vile deeds were what she had vowed to purge;
And though she did not know exactly how,
She would find the means that would not allow
The barons and their ilk to run amok.
Right now, daring was needed - and some luck.
She called a war council into session;
They voted to halt this foul oppression.

In minutes, the council had made fair plans
To rescue the doomed pair from Philip's hands.
Their bold plan involved a double attack.
They also aimed Philip's strong room to sack:
To relieve the earl of his gold and coin.
"Relieve," joked the Maiden, "But not purloin
For Philip did not his riches attain
Except through theft and inflicting great pain."
Two groups would separately make their way
Disguised as peasants come for market day.

The Maiden thrilled to dress like a rank hag;
On her head, she wore an old, filthy rag,
Which stank and hid from sight her shining hair.
While the rescue team was under her care,
Jonah was charged with the audacious raid

To liberate the gold. He shortly bade
His dear friends adieu and, in merchant's guise,
Left on his own for town to best apprise
Himself of the hated earl's resources.
The rest came next day on panting horses.

Jonah slowly explored the town's by-ways,
Looking like he'd ridden dusty highways.
In an alley, he found a grim tavern;
Its dark bar felt like a dripping cavern.
A curt, one-eyed wench sold beer and cider.
No one heeded this tall, burly rider
Who fed his horse in the tavern stable
And sat down at a worn, pock-marked table
Near a mute, cowled monk who simply nodded
And spoke up only when gently prodded:

"Brother, what dishes here are fit to eat?
I crave venison or some boiled pig's feet.
Art thou partial to roast mutton or fowl?
Is that a smile lurking behind your scowl?
Wouldst thou partake of a small, steaming cup?"
The gloomy monk visibly brightened up.
This good cleric took many more than one
And cost a goodly sum ere he was done.
His frozen tongue warmed by cider and ale,
He recounted for Jonah a strange tale.

His father was for years a castle smith;
Of ten close-spaced children, he was the fifth.
His mother he lost when he was quite young.
His stepmother a shrew with biting tongue,
Who swore at his father all too roundly
And, with a broom, beat the children soundly.
She was a widow with three howling brats,
Always bothering him like buzzing gnats.
She gave her precious own the choicest food
And lambasted poor Tom if he were rude.

Of some grievous sin, he was once accused
While his father, looking chagrined, excused
Himself and without a fuss, disappeared.
Towards nightfall - dead drunk - he reappeared
And, muttering nonsense, fell sound asleep.
From this, no fruitful harvest can one reap.
Tom's comrades now came from the meaner sort
Who kept barely free of the hundreds court.
They stole ripe apples from a blind man's stall
And, from a tree, hung a funeral pall.

Rubbing a plump sow with grease and rank grass,
They set her loose during mid-morning mass
But did not stay to watch the cursing priest,
With cassock flapping, chase the squealing beast.
The bailiff spoke wisely to Tom's father
Who cuffed the glum boy but did not bother
To put down his tankard of foaming beer
While his lips curled in a simpering leer.
The lad continued his droll pranks apace;
With doom, he was running a losing race.

The sheriff gave him a final warning;
Tom fled from home the very next morning.
For three months, he wandered the county roads,
Begging, stealing or carting heavy loads.
He fell in one day with a band of thieves
Who poached under the noses of dull reeves
Until one day red-handed they were caught
And before an enraged seignior were brought.
He proclaimed that, at dawn, they would be hung
And, into one large grave, their corpses flung.

A kind friar prevented Tom's demise:
"Hanging youngsters is a sin in God's eyes."
The good friar took Tom under his wing
And taught him to say daily prayers and sing
To the greater glory of God on high.

Tom finished his story with a deep sigh:
"I owe my soul to that godly friar
Who rescued me from Hell's eternal fire."
They talked until they heard the midnight bell.
It seemed that the monk knew the castle well

For to Philip's minions, he often preached,
Hoping that in some way, their souls he reached.
"As a past sinner, who am I to judge?
Their hope for redemption should I begrudge?
I know Philip to be unsavory;
He will one day walk his own Calvary."
"Shall we now," asked Jonah. "Talk man to man?"
He described in detail his cunning plan
To raid the strong room at the very hour
When the couple is led from the tower

For their beheading in the market square.
"Philip's men in armor will all be there
Leaving only a meager castle guard.
This coup will be fit subject for a bard.
My soldiers will arrive in town at dawn,"
He said, fighting vainly the urge to yawn.
The monk smiled and agreed to serve as guide;
He was the sort in whom you could confide.
"But what of the unhappy couple's fate?
Can aught be done afore it is too late?"

"We must in mighty Jehovah believe.
Their agony, I hope, He will relieve."
Tom regarded Jonah slightly askance:
"Art thou keeping some deep secret, perchance?
No matter, 'tis time for a few hours' rest.
Tomorrow, we may find ourselves hard-pressed.
I see you are not of the Christian church;
But all are one in the arduous search
For love, salvation and omniscient God
Until we lie beneath a grassy sod."

So saying, the monk lay down on a bench.
Jonah softly approached the one-eyed wench.
"Annabelle has spoken kindly of you.
Do you think you could get a message through?"

The Maiden's soldiers filtered into town
And divided into groups up and down
The square. Blending in with the market crowd,
They inspected trinkets and laughed out loud.
Their horses were held in a nearby wood
Where William and a score of archers stood.
Jonah's troops loaded a cart with gammon,
Ready for the watchmen to examine.
Tom and Jonah met them near the south gate
Which swung open just as the bell struck eight.

Philip and two score knights in measured ranks
Ushered forth as a balding priest gave thanks
For the blessings of Philip's gentle rule.
This venal hireling was no simple fool
But had a handsome share of Philip's loot.
The bystanders meanwhile stood wisely mute
As the lovers, hands bound behind their backs,
Strode to meet the executioner's axe.
With dignity they walked, their heads held high;
There were few that morning whose eyes were dry.

Jonah led his party past a gantry
And left the hams at the kitchen pantry.

Some old walls were being renovated.
Their presence was not investigated.
Tom led them through high-ceilinged, drafty halls
With tapestries adorning clammy walls.
Scenes of dying men and broken lances
Amidst rolling hills and quiet manses
Looked down on Jonah's troops as if to ask:
"For what purpose do you pursue this task?"

The monk led them down a dank corridor,
Which reached, at the north end, the strong room door.
Two guards, in the throes of sleep, were dispatched
To a fate with which they were rightly matched.
Neither guard had carried a strong room key.
"Hell's fire," said Tom. "This I did not foresee."
"Pray let me present a tinker's jewels,"
Chuckled Jonah showing a bag of tools.
The strong room was opened quick as a wink -
Before the incredulous monk could blink.

They entered the dim room in silent awe,
Gaping in disbelief at what they saw.
Bulging sacks of coins were arranged in rows
Like well-copied lines of elegant prose.
Tables were laden with jeweled caskets;
Strings of creamy pearls spilled from straw baskets.
There were boxes enough with precious stones
To repay the King's intemperate loans
That he spent on splendiferous tourneys,
Epicurean feasts and court journeys.

"This," said Jonah. "Explains our misery.
When seeing this, what crime is usury?"
The raiders carried a load down the stairs,
Then hurried back for additional wares.
Tom volunteered to guard the creaking cart;
He was a good monk of generous heart.
The second load did not take them as long;

But when they reached the yard, the cart was gone.
"Oh ye villainous monk and callous thief,"
Cursed Alice. "See how we are come to grief!"

Jonah spoke with no apparent concern:
"The scoundrel has done us no wicked turn.
Three of ours await him at the portal;
I trust in God but nary a mortal,"
Laughed Jonah as he heaved a weighty bag.
"Let us join that counterfeit, ill-dressed hag
Who is on the verge of striking her blow.
Carry what you can and let the rest go.
The devious monk will feel much oppressed
When, his treacherous folly, soon confessed,

We'll deal with kindly and so instruct him
How, in wiser fashion, his sails to trim.
My, how I do love a pithy proverb
Nor have I yet learned my wry tongue to curb."
At that moment, arose a shrill clamor
Of shouts and screams, of sword striking hammer.
Jonah's band broke into a headlong run,
Fearing to miss the fray - and all the fun.

The procession soon reached the crowded square.
The Maiden had placed her soldiers with care.
Philip's men-at-arms had marched down mute streets,
With the only sound: ominous drumbeats.
A mourning crowd waited to let them pass;
Philip's priest intoned a funeral mass.

The doomed couple was calm and dignified;
With deep love, their resolve was fortified.
A platform waited with pennants flying:
A stark thing sporting grim tools for dying.

On the platform rested a blood-stained block;
Seeing it gave the couple a nasty shock.
His face hidden behind an opaque mask,
The ax man awaited his gruesome task.
His dark eyes were calm and unrevealing.
To Philip, there was no use appealing
So they mounted the few steps side by side.
Their hands entwined, they neither spoke nor cried
But stood in steadfast peace, heads bowed in prayer
Until they took a last, deep gulp of air.

The executioner raised high his axe
But then stopped quite suddenly in his tracks
And let go the deadly axe with a start
As a sharp arrow pierced him through the heart.
His unrevealing eyes went cold and dead;
He would never cut off another head.
Then chaos in the tense square exploded
As the Maiden and her troops unloaded
Their righteous fury on Philip's minions.
Swords were drawn from ragged smocks and aprons.

The knights reacted with unfeigned surprise
To be struck by troops in plebeian guise.
One knight shouted: "God's blood, is this a joke?
To face swords in the hands of common folk."
Short-lived, sad to say, was his noxious jibe;
His windpipe was slashed by a former scribe.
The Maiden swung her bloodied sword about
While prodding her troops with a piercing shout:
"In the name of divine justice, attack -
Showing no quarter nor giving them slack!"

Sword and ax clashed one upon the other
As the crowd, in terror, ran for shelter.
The Maiden brandished her death-dealing sword;
Blood, from a badly wounded arm, then poured.
The air was shrill with grunts and awful groans,
The sounds of heaving lungs and cracking bones.
Back and forth, the fierce battle raged and churned;
Many were the market stalls overturned.
Strong hands meanwhile lifted the couple down
And spirited them quickly out of town.

The Maiden's forces over time gained sway,
Helped as Jonah's band rushed into the fray.
Hurling curses, Philip beat a retreat
And regrouped his knights in a narrow street.
In outraged tones, Philip harangued his men,
Commanding the cowards to charge again.
As his sharp tongue grew increasingly hot,
The contents of a brimming chamber pot
Were scornfully flung from a high dormer
To cleanse once strutting knights of their former

Vainglory. "Piss on ye," cried an old toad.
"Ye deserve prodding with a cattle goad
And dunking in the nearest foul sewer
To stink then of more than your own manure.
Brave enough at harassing poor widows,
Look how ye squiggle like frightened minnows
When faced with soldiers by God's justice armed.
Be sure that you leave this old head unharmed.
Come up here now and kiss my wrinkled ass
And step aside to let brave women pass."

Thus, the harridan cackled insanely
Through rotted teeth as the wet knights vainly
Swore, and cruel Philip was heard to roar:
"We'll return soon for you, you barren whore;
But for now, I have bigger fish to fry.

I want that proud Maiden hung out to dry."
Philip's men, insulted in their honor,
Charged forward for victory to garner.
The Maiden meanwhile pulled back her forces
And went to retrieve the waiting horses.

The old harridan thought it best to flee
And seek other lodgings and sights to see.
Her spiteful tongue had worked enough today;
She would need all her luck to get away.
As she stepped outside, she met a barmaid
With one eye and a scar that would not fade.
The barmaid whispered into Jenny's ear
Wise words the old lady was glad to hear.
The beautiful maid winked her one good eye,
Like a smiling fox and perhaps as sly.

Philip's howling knights pursued the Maiden
To face the arrows of William's bowmen.
The dense hale of arrows flew straight and fast;
Philip's harsh tyranny will soon be past.
Many of his knights lay dead on the field.
Philip fled, but his fate would now be sealed.
The remnants of his tired force staggered back,
Too disheartened for a renewed attack.
From the copse, the Maiden watched them depart,
Then knelt down to thank God with all her heart

For a victory at such modest cost:
Three fighters with light wounds but no one lost.
A learned doctor had joined her staff,
A rotund fellow with a hearty laugh.
Always ready with a wry witticism,
Of his healing, he brooked no criticism.
His trade was learned at university -
His art from knowledge of adversity.
And skill, from both, he could always summon.
He treated the sick, noble or common.

He had the darting eyes of an urchin;
His hands were calm as befits a surgeon.
Added to medical ability,
He could use a sword with facility.
He bound each wound with a clean linen wrap,
Turning to the Maiden to doff his cap.
She responded with a heart-warming smile:
"Let us ride home to camp and rest awhile.
Our bold exertions have today borne fruit;
There will soon be others to follow suit."

The Maiden nudged the mare and headed west.
Her victorious troops had earned their rest.
The rescued couple hurried alongside
To accord her thanks, but not without pride.
"And what will happen to our children now?"
"Surely," was her reply. "They will somehow
Keep themselves busy in our sylvan camp.
Be sure they take care in the cold and damp."
They looked at her in absolute surprise;
The Maiden had a twinkle in her eyes:

"I thought such a precaution well-advised;
Your complete concurrence I had surmised.
Two well-armed women made a quick foray;
Your courageous brother showed them the way.
Your fine children are eager, I feel sure,
To rush into your arms and be the cure
For the agonies you have just endured.
Your happiness, I trust, is now ensured."
Were there ever two quite so thunderstruck:
With mouths wide open but tongues that were stuck?

The Maiden urged Flame to a steady trot.
"Shall we find out what cook has in the pot?"
A good day's work, thought Flame, growing queasy;
Next time, I doubt, will be quite so easy.

XII

 Veritable Feast of Plots

The night was black and heavy with thunder;
Jagged lightning tore the sky asunder.
Sheets of rain cascaded like waterfalls,
And beat like fists upon the castle walls.
One fierce bolt split an oak almost in half.
A ragged peasant clutched a mewling calf
And struggled down a wind-swept village lane
With swirls of muddy water in her train.
Swallows and larks sheltered in tall church spires
While tired peasants huddled by crackling fires.

Their primitive huts had roofs tightly thatched;
Under the eaves, baby sparrows were hatched.
On the mud walls hung long wooden ladles;
Hungry babies cried in rough-hewn cradles.
Anxious mothers hushed them at swollen breasts
And waited in fear for unwelcome guests.
In the dread night, malignant spirits roamed:
Ghosts and fanged werewolves whose scarlet mouths foamed.
Eager to frighten weak souls that had sinned,
Devils raced through the night on a foul wind.

Drenched guards on the slippery ramparts cursed,
Their frayed nerves seared by every thunder burst.
The long day's travel had left them weary -
The least sound a danger in theory.
Their joints were stiff, and their clothing was soaked.
One comfort: too much rain for ghosts, they joked.
Three burly guards sheltered beneath an arch,
Complaining about the day's endless march.
"I've ne'er seen the King in such a hurry.
Did you see those blasted peasants scurry?"

"My aching, blistered feet are oozing pus;
That Captain Roger is a bloody cuss."
"Passing village after stinking village,
And only one did he let us pillage.
With barely time to snatch a yearling pig,
This royal progress may not yield a fig!"
"What a dangerous mood the King is in!
I wonder when the fighting will begin."
"As soon as we find that ragtag army,
We'll grind it finer than pork salami

And swing the Maiden from a sturdy tree.
The survivors: enslave – though few there be!"
"Bloody true," said the third praetorian.
"This is no place for a Gregorian.
The grim field of Mars will be burnished red
And fetid with the corpses of their dead.
A broad, crimson tide will untrammeled flow;
Their eyeballs will be eaten by a crow.
Their bodies will be raked by savage paws,
And their insides will hang from hungry maws."

In the storm-blasted night, a lone wolf howled;
Two of the guards shivered; the other scowled.
The blood-thirsty braggart's face blanched with fear;
And he whispered hoarsely, this craven seer:
"The Maiden, by report, keeps a werewolf,
Befriends wild beasts and teaches Beowulf.
Cutthroats and thieves she hangs by the dozen:
God's holy truth, sworn by my third cousin
Who was told it by a money lender,
Who, in turn, heard it from a fruit vendor,

Who, if truth be known, was betimes informed
By a drunken friar, now much reformed,
Who ... "At which interval, the scowling guard
Hissed at them in a manner rough and hard:
"God curse each of you as a prating fool,

With toothless gums and gaping mouths that drool.
Ye jump at sounds and each leaf that quivers;
A beaten dog howls, you get the shivers.
What mockery will ye be in battle
Where the clash of arms o'er whelms pale prattle."

The slanting rain now turned to gentle drops
While on the ramparts strolled two seeming fops
Discoursing on the marvels of the night
And quoting poetry with all their might.
"Look yonder: such is what makes a dandy:
Garbed in fashion and spouting poetry.
The harsh din of battle will have them quake.
What sort of useless men does God now make?"
Furiously, the guard spat as was meet,
The fat globule hitting Sir Roger's feet.

The guard fell silent to no one's surprise
And bowed contritely to apologize.
The captain cursed them for worthless chattel,
Needing such prodding as grazing cattle.
He gave with his broadsword a vicious blow
To the first guard and bade him quickly go
Back to his own post to conclude his watch.
This simple duty he better not botch;
For should he from sloth chance to fall asleep,
He would Satan's company shortly keep.

The two left fell under the same duress.
Sir Roger's mailed fist was no soft caress
Of a lover intending to persuade;
Of lazy scoundrels he was not afraid.
The truant guards scurried to their places,
Abject terror stamped upon their faces.
The two fashionable strollers passed by,
And Sir Roger addressed them with a sigh:
"Three slackers, Your Grace, needing discipline."
England's High Constable said with a grin:

"Your vigilance, Captain, is commended
And in no manner should be amended.
The enemies of our King are legion
And doubtless infest this very region.
A love of justice, they are wont to feign;
But in John's stead, they dearly thirst to reign –
A thirst that high power alone can slake,
Which, if sated, will give our oak a shake
And rain on our heads most foul disorders.
They are nothing short of vile marauders.

The power of the King is absolute,
In which defense we must stand resolute.
By divine authority our kings rule.
Those who seek to rebel are but the tool
Of the Devil's host of fiendish warlocks
Who pull our trim beards and tweak our forelocks.
These witches are full of devilish tricks,
Tormenting us with unseen stones and sticks.
They amuse their master at our expense,
Our only protection: God's providence.

Blackest of these rebels is this Maiden
Who in treachery is Satan's maven.
Blood she sips from a pure silver chalice;
Her heart overflows with wicked malice.
Her vaunted cause for us no good portends;
Chaos would result from what she intends.
From obedience, the peasants would stray;
Their just taxes, she tells serfs not to pay.
To labor is the serf's moral duty;
For us, the contemplation of beauty.

So, good Sir Roger, maintain your sternest;
This combat will be in deadly earnest."
The knight crisply bowed and his best vouchsafed,
Stating with force that at the bit, he chafed.
Dismissing Sir Roger with a curt wave,

The Constable wished the others so brave.
Then to his companion in a low tone;
"Our venal King will reap as he has sown;
His depredations are too much to bear.
The crown, I shall before much longer, wear.

But first, of the Maiden, we must dispose;
Or else, I shall have but fleeting repose
And rule a fractious kingdom torn in two.
The Maiden dies before our plot is through."
The Constable's friend responded in kind:
"Is sly Count Gerard of similar mind?"
"I care not a whit if he be or not;
His life is forfeit to our modest plot.
The Maiden has Gerard most rightly cursed;
She'll hang him, except she'll quarter him first.

His sanguine deeds have proved all too grievous:
His exactions surpassing onerous.
My vassals I rule with a steady hand,
But neither burn their homes nor steal their land.
Without peasant crops, how would earls get fed?
The wheat and rye they grow becomes our bread.
All unruly serfs must be kept in line,
To work and provide what is duly mine.
Dispossessed peasants take to the highways
And threaten the calm meter of our days."

"How do we rid ourselves of this King John?"
Questioned Stephen of Kent, trembling and wan.
"Mark you how richly the King likes to sup.
At a holiday feast, a poisoned cup
Will serve our hidden purpose passing well
And speed good King John on his way to Hell.
With both John and the Maiden neatly gone,
The crown will come to me before too long.
The loyal barons will not long resist.
Chopping off a head or two may assist

Them to speak clearly with a single voice,
Confirming me as their favorite choice."
"My Lord, you have in truth a subtle wit."
"Think ye so? Shall we go and by John sit?"
At this, Greek Zeus aimed his bolts. The rain poured,
And Roman Jupiter in outrage roared.
The small, woodland creatures ran for cover;
And dark spirits in the night did hover.

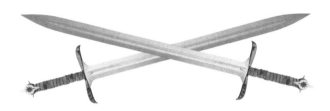

Four men in furs stood near a blazing fire,
Gathered in an oak-beamed hall to conspire.
Gerard stood a bit taller than the rest;
He wore a dagger with a handsome crest.
Philip the Cruel had lost weight – and stank;
He put a goblet to his lips and drank.
The somber Duke of Essex stroked his beard;
He was, of all four, the most greatly feared.
The King sported a fancy, velvet cap;
He studied with care a crudely drawn map.

"Somewhere in Great Blaxford is where they hide;
To fight in those woods would be suicide.
We must devise a bait with which to lure
Them to a battle on the open moor
Where our well-trained knights will crush them with ease.
Their wounded will swing gently in the breeze,
Their eyes bulging and their tongues distended.
For such deeds was I from birth intended."
King John's voice echoed through the vaulted hall.
An incomplete portrait hung on the wall.

"What a lovely portrait of the Duchess:
Precise in proportion, a true likeness.
But pray tell me," said John with a wry smile.
"Did she despair from sitting such a while?
Or was some unpaid scoundrel having fun?
For this fine painting was left quite undone."
"A wicked wench, Sire, an evil strumpet;
She fled before I could sound the trumpet
And joined the Maiden in her woodland dell.
Skilled in a shrewd craft is this Annabelle."

King John smiled slyly and began to speak
When into the hall burst a gruesome freak.
He was an ugly gnome of no great height,
With a bulbous head – an outlandish sight.
Red-veined was his thick nose from love of drink;
From hard swearing, he was not one to shrink.
Coarse tufts of hair sprouted from longish ears.
His cynic's wit, he turned on fools and peers.
His hot tongue over a cool mind prevailed;
And to avoid sarcasm, he always failed.

Roderick – a name that outdid his size –
Addressed John in a manner most unwise.
"Most mighty monarch, of England master,
Whose fame and fabled fortune grows faster
Than a still hummingbird can beat her wings,
Than a viper envenoms when she stings,
Than Apollo rides on his daily course,
Than Cupid's bold arrow can spend its force,
Whose character is so widely revered,
Whose retribution is so justly feared,

In whom cold logic and hot love dispute
And the wisdom of whose gnomes, few refute;
What then is amiss in your royal house
Where lords scurry through brush like molting grouse?
As rank weeds have spring flowers over grown

Or howling winds have grave disaster sown,
Word of this Maiden, like a fisher's net
Cast over the swollen and briny wet,
Has reaped a grim harvest of discontent
And, unabated, shall your kingdom rent.

Thou art indeed a most merry monarch,
Whirling over fields like a meadow lark.
To hunt, to dance, to dress in smart fashion:
Herein lies your veritable passion.
Hast thou not ears to hear nor eyes to see
Thy subjects' ever-growing misery?
Thy taxes are a monument to greed.
Havoc alone grows from such monstrous seed.
If you wish to draw the Maiden's sharp sting,
Then peace and prosperity must you bring

To this bitter land where turmoil now reigns,
Fomented by barons with pea-sized brains.
Indeed, what cunning fellows have we here?
Do they cook a plot or offer good cheer?
Sire, why consort with such villains as these?
Rather, find a consort who will thee please;
Or if no honest maid will thee marry,
At least with honest men pray thee tarry!"
"Enough," cried John. "Hold thy venomous tongue;
Or by mine own hands, thy fat neck be wrung."

The gnome, with a shriek, leaped high in the air,
Tumbled backwards and safely landed fair
On his dwarfish feet. "Sire, you surely jest.
I would prefer that dagger with a crest
But wonder how yon fine Count came by it:
Begging, stealing or his murderous wit."
Blanching, Gerard drew the crested dagger.
Roderick screamed, pretending to stagger:
"Help me quickly, Sire, else I be murdered.
Whose disloyal quest will then be furthered?

What false chaos will engulf the kingdom?
Who would then give tuppence for a dukedom?
I alone tell thee the truth unvarnished
And with neither herbs nor spices garnished.
Your Highness, take me for a prating fool,
Who can never abide the simplest rule:
A spiteful gnome telling more than he knows
And yet perceives not how the rude wind blows.
I beg thee spare me from this cold knight's ire:
His baleful heart of ice, his eyes of fire.

Look there how his burning ears pour out smoke;
He'll slice through my throat with a single stroke."
Roderick knelt down in supplication.
John laughed at the dwarf's wry fabrication
And started to command Gerard refrain,
But his words were drowned in a cry of pain
As the honed dagger pierced Roderick's chest.
"How do you like that for a clever jest?"
Sneered Count Gerard as the gnome struck the floor.
A last gurgle and he was heard no more.

Gerard viewed the dead body with distaste:
"My Lords, we have no further time to waste
On sorry jesters and rude curmudgeons.
That is why castles have lovely dungeons.
Why, I have in mine an exquisite wheel
From which the bravest man cannot conceal
The deeply hidden secrets of his heart
'Ere the soul from his body doth depart.
May I suggest we now discuss as planned
The royal business we had well in hand

Until we endured a gross disturbance
By this wordy, wart-nosed, peevish nuisance?"
The King's command caused two slaves to appear
To cart Roderick to a shabby bier.
The King, for a mere instant, looked distraught,

Then calmly spoke in phrases clearly wrought:
"I shall repeat what I said just before.
Our skilled knights can, in open country, gore
Her army like a furious, trapped bear
(Which roars fierce defiance mixed with despair

While savage dogs in a bloodthirsty pack
With dripping fangs attack it front and back)
Falls victim to a blind, relentless wrath
Even having ripped a few dogs in half.
What then, my lords, shall be our sly deceit
With which to gull this maid in her conceit?"
"Why my liege," quoth Gerard. "How like you this?
Here lies a cunning plan with naught amiss.
The Maiden reveres her home ancestral
As a parish priest his dog-eared missal;

And she will surely go to any length,
Howsoever it might confound her strength,
To save the remnant of the old estate.
It is thus she will meet her wretched fate.
You must select a closely trusted spy
With an honest face but the skill to lie.
This brave man must be completely loyal
And devoted to the power royal.
Disguised as a lowly castle scullion,
Reeking of stale garlic and raw onion,

(The pungent relics of the kitchen trade),
He'll carry a tale to this errant maid
That he shall report to have overheard
As the midnight watch ate a roasted bird.
'Tis a tale that is sure to strike a spark
And make of our Maiden an easy mark:
A tale of my intended knavery
To burn her fields and into slavery
Sell all the peasants including children.
And thus, we'll trap this bothersome Maiden."

The King bethought himself for a moment,
Thick fingers plucking his silken garment.
A wicked smile played on his tumid lips
As he stroked his chin with his fingertips.
"I have a brazen slave who'll do the trick:
Youthful and learns anything in a nick."
King John gave a lackey a sharp command
And, back to the fire, waited chin in hand.
Through the archway stepped a dazzling beauty
Who knelt gravely to the King on one knee.

"Sarafina, you have sought your freedom;
We need your services for the kingdom."

XIII

rmond

A band of knights through the dense forest rode;
Their pennons rippled, their bright armor glowed.
Huge chargers snorted as they trod the earth,
Straining at their long bits to show their worth.
The knights rode quietly in even pairs,
Speaking in French of far distant affairs.
"Je pense souvent de Paris maintenant.
Me demande si j'ai un deuxieme enfant."
"Le roi veut commencer encore une guerre,
Mais c'est a lui; ce n'est point mon affaire."

"Quel pays ridicule, surtout la cuisine;
Ce que je manque plus, c'est une bonne terrine."
Their topics, like the clouds, slowly drifted
As their moods by tiny inches shifted.
Trotting at first across wide, grassy downs -
With not a village, much less any towns,
They rode fast under a broad English sky,
Watched in silence by the few passersby.
But in time the forest wrapped around them
Like a wild vine twines round a growing stem.

Branches formed twisted patterns overhead,
And outlandish sounds caused increasing dread.
"Sacre Dieu, c'est un foret plus que noir;
Il y a des choses etranges on peut pas voir."
They spoke thus in a manner sore perplexed.
The goblins here have more than one man vexed.
Spirits abound of every type and sort.
Shades dismal and rapturous both cavort
To the ghostly notes of courtly music.
This ether shelters the tongue-tied rustic,

The dull apprentice asleep in the straw,
The rotund, greedy clerk stuffed to the craw,
The kind abbess in supplicating prayer,
The damsel riding a sure-footed mare,
A smithy, his forehead beaded with sweat,
The barren miser, not one to forget
Each farthing spent on a lamb or a shoat,
The shy beggar in someone's worn out coat,
A proud bishop carrying his crosier,
A fuller, a spinner, and a hosier.

Mischievous beings crowd the lucent air,
Dancing on noses and hiding in hair.
Elves, goblins, fairies and sprites by the score:
Some amusing, others worse than a bore.
Some had formerly known an earthly life;
But others, with which the dense air is rife,
Have known only an insubstantial world.
They weep to see human folly unfurled
Like a flag that catches each passing wind.
Only vain man does God's great love rescind.

Two woodland sprites began a rousing dance,
Unseen, unheard by these fair knights of France.
Their gossamer gowns rose and gently fell,
Shimmering with light and weaving a spell.
They reached for distant stars on elfin toes -
Hung in the air, and for an instant, froze.
They slid through the clouds in a long glissade -
The wind their stage, the dark trees a facade.
The dance ended, they took numerous bows
And ambled off on miniature cows.

A host of elves raised a flowered maypole;
Perched on top was a departed queen's soul.
She whistled and clapped her ringed hands with glee
Watching the elves dancing furiously.
They waved hued ribbons as they whirled around

The slender pole raised ten feet from the ground.
Primrose garlands wreathed their delicate heads
While purple clover bloomed in airy beds,
And juniper wafted a fragrant scent
That tickled noses from Devon to Kent.

A long, incorporeal trumpet blared
As serried ranks of honeysuckle flared.
Rows upon rows of bells in consort rang;
A chorus of shades hallelujahs sang.
The swarming multitudes grew strangely still,
And gentle murmurings replaced the shrill
But joyous cries of whirling, dancing sprites
And the vain boasts of long-departed knights.
With pomp advanced a sprightly procession:
A royal court returning from session.

First approached the radiant elfin Queen,
Gowned from head to toe in emerald green,
With the elfin King floating at her side.
They had that morning taken a brisk ride
Through the wide universe and briny seas
On tame seahorses and gigantic bees.
The Queen reveled in the raucous acclaim.
Her jovial husband felt much the same.
Their merry chatter the sprites now resumed
And a lavish feast avidly consumed.

They dined on dried toads' ears and spiced bats' wings
Baked in a pie with beets and such fine things
As worms and grubs for a touch of flavor.
The grasshopper soup to fully savor,
They delicately sipped like a fine wine
Imported from the Moselle or the Rhine.
The main course of hairy spider and beans
Was followed by boiled dandelion greens
Garnished with beetles, acorns and fish scales -
Not to forget nuts and diced lizard tails.

The French knights trotted along undeterred;
The wraithlike goblins they perhaps inferred.
At their head rode an imposing figure,
Looking every inch the august seigneur;
But he was not an earl or haughty lord.
A wise man: he was by many adored.
"Halt!" An armed woman stepped into their path.
"Proceed no further, or ye know our wrath!"
Each startled French knight drew his tempered arm.
Annabelle then spoke with endearing charm:

"Before you strike, I pray you look about;
It would be, I fear, a most gruesome rout."
Grim-faced men and women, their bows drawn tight,
Could be seen sitting on limbs at great height.
More archers stepped out from behind broad trees,
Aiming their arrows at the horses' knees.
Egbert's fighters came forward, fifty strong;
Each had a broadsword or battle ax drawn.
The calm French leader moved forward a pace
To look Annabelle squarely in the face:

"We desire no more than to pass in peace;
If denied, we shall fight without surcease.
And though we all perish, we doubtless will
Play much havoc and many surely kill.
Limbs shall we sever, the earth make bloody;
On these sanguine themes, I beg you study."
This Frenchman spoke his English passing well,
Smiling most affably at Annabelle.
"Ormond! Pray God my eyes do not deceive!
Put up your weapons so that none may grieve!"

Commanded the Maiden, not concealing
A joyous grin and emotions reeling.
She rode up to Ormond and grasped his hand,
Raising it high in a manner quite grand:
"Welcome, dear friends, from across the wild sea

To join our cause and share our victory!"
Only a few noticed her tears break out
Since just then was heard a clamorous shout:
"Robert! Robert!" Pierre burst out of the crowd.
"Mon petit frere!" he cried in a voice loud

Enough so that all that were gathered there
Warmly cheered and sang out: *"Mon petit frere!"*
And then a round of frenzied mirth took place
As English bluster met Parisian grace.

XIV

The Charter and a Declaration

Under the stars, a sylvan feast was held.
To stoke the fires, a thick-branched oak was felled.
Platters piled high with crisply roasted fowl
(Boar's tongue, shank of roebuck and fat hog's jowl)
Were carried around many blazing fires,
Which made of the treetops shadowy spires.
Bowls of apples and pears stacked in tall mounds,
Crusty loaves each weighing several pounds,
And earthy cheeses – all straight from the farm -
Were served by a man with one severed arm,

Cut off for some abominable deed
Like stealing bread for his children to feed.
The Brave Maiden sheltered all and sundry,
Leaving no man or beast to go hungry.
Pies and cakes in forms multitudinous
Left many fingers stained and glutinous.
Singing and frenzied dancing soon ensued,
For the entire company was imbued
With a noisy spirit of fun and hope.
Is this, thought Flame, a visit from the Pope?

The Maiden and wise Ormond walked apart,
Speaking of sad matters that touched each heart.
She told him what happened that dreadful day,
Of the vow made when she had knelt to pray.
She spoke of the great cause undertaken,
How she would feel lonely and forsaken
But also of the joy of her stout band -
Sworn to restore peace to this ravaged land.
She described how the tiny band had grown,
How the first seeds of justice had been sown.

Her voice broke, speaking of her family.
Ormond then mentioned the word destiny.
Dispatches had reached him in rugged Wales
That caused him to run up wide canvas sails
And try in France careful diplomacy,
An occupation much like minstrelsy.
"How often have I hurled deprecations,
At times so ripe with prevarications
That such a monster could slay your Father,
And no baron even seemed to bother.

For the others, my rent heart grieves no less,
Not least thy Mother's worthy damsel Tess,
Whom I had eagerly hoped to marry.
On such thoughts, it were best not to tarry."
Gently touching his arm, the Maiden sighed
And wiped a falling tear she wished to hide.
"Ormond, dear friend, were my poor wits so slow:
To see you both talking and not to know?"
"Ah, Milady, we must have our secrets;
For mine, I feel sorrow but no regrets."

Ormond allowed himself a wistful smile.
"But now we have no more time to beguile,"
He said drawing from beneath his long cloak
A parchment scroll embossed with a broad oak.
Unrolling the parchment for her to read,
He said that within it lay a small seed
From which a formidable tree would grow.
This seed, no matter what ill winds may blow,
Will inspire justice if it be nourished.
"As in lofty Athens, freedom flourished;

So this is a bold stroke to set men free
By limiting our puissant monarchy.
Establishing the rights of each estate
And the various duties owed the state,
This plan will unlimber the crushing yoke

Weighing now on both lords and common folk.
Herein we read many a principle
To make a just people invincible.
We here see created sound government
With courts, offices and a parliament

Without whose consent, no laws will be made
Neither customs levied nor taxes paid.
Reflect on this as a good beginning:
A rough, tangled wool that needs much spinning
Before an elegant cloth be woven,
A timber as yet by axe uncloven,
Which wants some dressing before set in joints
To construct a building of finer points.
Your Father called this script the Great Charter.
It was long his ardent wish to barter

With the King to revise the old regime.
And while he held this King in low esteem,
He believed the Great Charter would provide
A peaceful path to avoid regicide."
This last spoken in a voice thin and hushed,
Ormond's serene face grew anxious and flushed.
"Such an action only in extremis
Should John prove to be stubborn and heedless.
The Charter will be your inheritance;
Your Father trusted in your common sense.

A kingdom, he said, based on decent laws
Will be spared the savage, relentless claws
Of violence and Godless anarchy.
He wanted a strong but wise monarchy
To build a land of broad prosperity:
A truly good and just society
Wherein men and women may till in peace,
Milk their bleating goats and sell bags of fleece
Without an arrogant lord's by-your-leave
Or greasing the palm of a taloned reeve.

Good laws are founded on common consent;
We eschew a monarch thought Heaven sent.
But we need a king fair-minded and strong
Because a feeble king can cause much wrong.
Study with knitted brows your Father's gift.
Worship it not; neither give it short shrift."
"Intrepid Ormond let me read it through
Whilst ye make new friends and savor cook's stew."
It was at this juncture that Sarah chose
To nudge the Maiden with her wolfish nose.

"I see the many rumors be not false.
To call this warm-hearted wolf a dog halts
At the frontier of imagination.
Yet as dog, she has some inclination.
Pray how came a wild beast to be so tame?"
"A story that merits not so much fame
But which I can share with thee in due course.
There works, in this wood, more than human force."

Ormond started to leave but paused instead;
He considered briefly, nodding his head:
"I see they know not who you really are.
Your followers have come with you this far
And so deserve to know the simple truth.
Your bearing shows such high and innate couth
That this report will be taken in stride.
From destiny, you cannot flee or hide."
Ormond nodded and then genuflected:
A gesture that she had not expected.

"Dear friend, I give you leave to so pronounce;
My secret, sad to say, I must renounce.
But Ormond, reprieve me an hour or two -
Until the early morning's rosy hue
Expels the roguish demons of the night.
Let me stay the Brave Maiden 'til first light."
Ormond understood and left her alone.

Standing near, only Will heard her low groan
As she thought of past days of innocence.
She trod this path with no small reticence.

A refreshing night breeze brushed by her cheek.
She knew there was a sceptered crown to seek
And prayed duty's ship would not run aground
On ambition's shoal with her siren sound.
The soothing breeze brushed by her cheek again.
She exclaimed: "By almighty God, I can."
William paced tensely near a fading fire,
Filled with his unbounded love and desire.
He beseeched the Maiden on bended knee:
"I beg thee to love if not marry me.

Long have I kept my yearning heart in check
And remained content to serve at your beck
And call. I firmly swore never to break
My wordless vigil, but this wrenching ache
I can no more endure but must declare
My humble love and most reverend prayer."
The Maiden felt a tear spring to her eye
And bent down to the wolf, fearing to cry.
"Oh William, thou art my beloved friend;
'Twould be a joy to have some common end.

But my heart, unlike the hawk, is not free;
Marry, I must, one of my own degree.
I shall love thee as I did my brother;
But for thee, my heart can bear no other
Love. Yet, rejoice, I have in mind a prize
That will dazzle many a damsel's eyes.
I mean to see thee most happily wed;
But patience, Will, for now enough is said."
"I will accept no other love but thine;
No earthly bloom can replace one divine."

"Dearest friend, act not such a wayward part.
Who gainsays the ambitions of the heart
May also deny our flat earth's fixed place
And observe in the moon no smiling face.
Such a man decries as an old wives' tale
The miracle of herbs that never fail
To cure the pox or Saint Vitus' mad dance.
At the alchemist's feats, he looks askance
And prides himself in the name of skeptic;
But he is instead a carping cynic.

Let not gracious love with pride be tarnished,
Nor a hopeful heart too quickly banished.
For the true course of love is never known,
And seldom are man's foolish ways outgrown."
Will, like a philosopher deep in thought,
Struggled to learn the lesson she had taught.
He left her company to lift his gaze
To heaven's splendors and wish for the day's
Quick beginning. He had enough to do,
And zealous work his spirits would renew.

The cold-banning fires were now burning low;
The embers gave off a shimmering glow.
Annabelle ate a pear with a sly grin;
A slight trickle of juice ran down her chin.
Hovering near her like a flame-drawn moth,
Pierre quickly offered a silk, damask cloth.
Annabelle smiled shyly and touched his cheek;
Pierre felt all at odds and suddenly meek.
There was a question he wanted to ask,
But silence enveloped him like a mask.

Hypnos now cast a wide, ensnaring net
Over travelers and new friends well met.
A dreamless fog of sleep immured them all,
And few got up to answer Nature's call.
Those that did saw an endless starry sky

And heard the faint notes of a cuckoo's cry.
How could they know what turn events would take,
Or what harsh fate would greet them at daybreak?
They went to sleep with the camp in order
And woke to find trouble and disorder.

Dawn spread slowly across the morning sky.
The Maiden woke in a mood gently wry.
She planned with Annabelle the day's affairs.
"How tasted last night those succulent pears?"
Asked the Maiden in an ironic voice.
"Quite sweet," was the reply. "They were most choice."
"Methinks you have found far more to admire
In pears than just their sweetness would require.
He is a brave and most courteous man;
Cupid's arrows follow no given plan."

"Truly milady, dost thou find him so?
I am so lost in love, I cannot know.
My heart is unanchored, my eyes gone blind;
Chaos reigns within my once steady mind.
I feel, with him, like the first day of spring
But failing in speech and where to begin.
I am also far below his station.
Would loving me stain his reputation?"
The Maiden gave a shudder at this last
As if struck by deep winter's icy blast.

"Some indeed may not wed below their rank."
At these hard words, Annabelle's spirits sank.
"But for some, it is an outmoded view
Put in place to serve the privileged few.
Pierre, I expect, will marry whom he wills
With scant regard for noble rank or frills.
But I would not taunt or keep you guessing
So know that you shall receive my blessing.
And now to take up some pressing business,
I saw yesterday a broken harness

And three costly swords in need of repair.
Pray see to these ere you taste the next pear."
Annabelle agreed, and her spirits rose;
But seeing Jonah's angry face, she froze.
"What report," asked the Maiden. "That disturbs
Your morning, and your placid humor curbs?"
"A poor scullery maid, the worse for wear,
Has taken flight from the King's beastly lair
With a tale that will cause your saints to rage
And be writ foul even in this harsh age.

Such enormity will curdle the milk
In a mother's breast. The King and his ilk
Alone could work such abomination
Whose horror exceeds imagination.
But enough, hither comes the tattered rag.
Let her relate whereof these villains brag."
Sarafina, her beauty hid by dirt,
Knelt before the Maiden in a torn shirt.
"Pity, oh great lady, this wretched cur;
I never meant to spoil his lordship's fur.

He had me beaten with a cat o'nine;
My gashes were treated with steaming brine."
Sobbing, she lifted her coarse shirt a crack
To reveal knotted welts across her back.
The Maiden let fly a furious oath.
Taking hold of Sarafina with both
Hands, she sought to know from this slender reed
What rank whoreson had done this evil deed.
Sarafina spoke in a rasping tone
That sounded almost like a dying moan:

"Noble Count Gerard with King John's consent.
I pleaded that it was an accident.
My pleas were in vain; he paid them no mind
And said I was lucky not to be fined."
Ormond had quietly joined the small group.

Listening hard, he let his shoulders droop.
The Maiden begged the poor wretch continue;
She felt a hot rage in every sinew.
"They set me to work carrying foul slops
And washing floors at night with tangled mops."

Pausing, she twisted her thick matted hair;
She smelt like a pig at a county fair.
"One night, I heard two scurrilous sergeants,
With mean, slitted eyes and mouths like rodents,
Boasting as they fed their sweating faces
How they would use their nail-studded maces
To crush the heads of the Maiden's peasants
And drive their children like hunted pheasants
Through the rolling hills and wooded valleys
To be sold as slaves on Turkish galleys.

When they had done with murder and pillage,
They had firm orders to burn her village.
The march, they said, began on the morrow
And would end in the Maiden's great sorrow.
I waited in a closet out of sight
And fled the castle just before first light.
Milady, I beg of you protection;
I am now a maid without connection."
"No harm shall befall thee in this safe place;
Get thee breakfast and wash thy sooty face.

Pray God ye have come to us in good time
To abort this vengeful and monstrous crime.
I admire thee for thy valiant spirit
And your escape from that evil ferret.
Much of our vaunted aristocracy
Does not rise above mediocrity.
They care for little but to dance and hunt -
Their speech no deeper than a wild boar's grunt.
Nobility comes from a worthy heart
And may well be found in a common tart.

The will to virtue and to right a wrong
Depends not if a fellow's purse be long."
"Milady, thinkest me a prostitute?
A humble maid am I, but resolute."
"I meant not to speak directly of thee,
But more in a broad generality.
Think nothing amiss nor further on it;
Keep safe thy courage and noble spirit."
Sarafina bowed low and backed away
As the Maiden said, "We shall leave today

And attain the village in three days' ride.
All details to Annabelle, I confide."
Ormond thoughtfully took off his soft cap:
"Something is not quite right; I smell a trap.
Her story is simply too convenient;
And while Count Gerard is never lenient,
To whip a lass with a cat- o'-nine-tails
(A punishment next which her error pales)
Is even for Gerard far too severe.
I suspect some vile trick is hidden here."

The Maiden reacted with great distress:
"Your thesis could be right; I cannot guess.
But certain I am that we must not wait
Else we incur the risk of being late.
And, therefore, let us promptly all to horse;
My mind once firmly set, so too my course.
To God and justice, let us pledge our swords.
From them alone, look we for our rewards."
Her companions nodded while she spoke low:
"Friend Jonah, a brief word before you go."

XV

attle

The burning sun felt like hot coals that noon.
Egbert whistled an ancient, dirge-like tune.
Horses were saddled and arrows counted;
Armor was fastened as soldiers mounted.
Bowstrings were tightly drawn and lances decked
With fluttering pennons. Axes were checked;
And swords, the mighty instruments of Mars,
Sparkled like the myriad distant stars.
Annabelle gave orders in a flurry,
Urging knights to saddle up and hurry.

The fighters were ready and assembled.
The Brave Maiden, at their head, resembled
A fierce warrior queen of ancient lore,
Fully mantled with the dour tools of war.
This diverse army of plebeian cast,
Culled like the fishes of the foaming vast
And trained in a calling 'til then unknown
(To them), had, from a tiny seed, now grown
To a force that could confront misery
And change the course of woeful history.

She surveyed this army fresh and eager,
Sprung from roots so clearly rough and meager,
And felt, mixed with pride, a hesitation:
Could she lead this rapid catenation
Or would events spin out of her control
And leave her shorn of her immortal soul?
A soft breeze stirred the stifling, humid air
Lifting from her shoulders a heavy care.
She briefly caught sight of the smiling fox
While her fingers played with her auburn locks.

She lifted high her sword and fiercely cried:
"Forward, dear friends, for neither gold nor pride
But to strike for justice a fervent blow.
We shall show mercy to the vanquished foe."
Lusty cheers resounded throughout the glen
Thrilling the hearts of brave women and men.
There is one, however, she sternly thought
Who will not survive our enraged onslaught.
Ormond now rode forward and raised his sword,
Requesting quiet from the cheering horde.

"Most excellent fighters, noble and brave,"
He addressed them in a voice calm yet grave.
"We fight to bring peace to a troubled land
And see justice served with an even hand.
The light of your deeds will forever burn,
But some who go today will not return.
She who has led you to honor and fame
Has from policy withheld her proud name;
So, before this bold journey doth begin,
Pray all bow to the Princess Gwendolyn,

Princess of the royal line and true heir
To haughty, unwed, barren John, whose fair
Sister was Mother to this brave princess.
The King has dark, grievous sins to confess.
So as further cause to our noble fight,
We boldly march to claim her distaff right
To succeed King John on proud England's throne.
John, for his vicious habits, must atone;
And while we hesitate in his demise,
He henceforth will rule justly – or he dies.

To that end, a wise charter has been writ
That binds him to rule - not as he sees fit -
But only with the estates' due consent.
It is a bold and wondrous document."
Ormond's speech sparked an uproarious din

With wild cries of "Gwendolyn! Gwendolyn!"
William's shock could not be considered mild;
The Princess nodded graciously and smiled.
"Milady … Your Highness … my impudence …"
"'Twas nothing, dear friend, but sound evidence

Of your prodigious love and high esteem
For me. May I prove worthy of your dream.
The pledge I made thee I shall not forget.
Now see that your sturdy archers are set
To march, for hard traveling lies ahead;
And we sup on naught but hard cheese and bread.
By day and night shall we swiftly travel
To catch the King and his plot unravel.
Like a sly cat, we rest in fleeting naps,
With a shrewd eye open for fiendish traps.

I hear John's dreaded minions are afoot.
To crush their power, we must firmly put
Every muscle and sinew to the wheel.
The danger we face, I cannot conceal.
But as brothers and sisters, we stand fast.
Now spur our horses, for the die is cast."
The Princess raised her mighty sword once more.
Her warriors responded with a roar;
And as the ear-splitting cheer reached the sky,
The army surged forward, weapons held high.

They rode through the forest for two full days
With spirits high and singing roundelays.
Annabelle and Pierre traveled together;
They wore in their caps a sprig of heather.
The twins, as always, argued merrily,
Stabbing the air with shouts of "verily".
William preceded his corps of marksmen,
Their ranks swelled with hardy men and women
Who could hit mid-flight a flying squirrel
Or cut from a necklace a gleaming pearl.

They emerged from the dark, purple shadows
To blink in the glare of sun-drenched meadows.
They trotted east along a narrow road
Seeing neither village nor thatched abode.
But soon, a galloping band of twenty
Men, raising dust and with arms aplenty,
Rode over a low crest and into sight.
They were led by a dashing, tousled knight.
"My beautiful warrior," he exclaimed.
"Your audacious spirit has not been tamed,

But this time you've brought an imposing force.
Might you care for another twenty horse?"
"I thought you had but a private motive
And that it would take more than a votive
Candle for you to fight out of season.
Our war, but for justice, has no reason."
"Milady, I have sought thee high and low
And raised a valiant troop in hopes to show
The deeper side of a complex nature.
Let your heart be judge and legislature,

And I will ask no more distinguished prize
Than a welcome look from thy flashing eyes."
"Welcome, then, to our beneficent cause;
We can now, however, no longer pause.
Ormond, prithee assign these men a place
Along our line." "With great pleasure, Your Grace."
The knight recoiled in disbelief and shock:
"Is this some wayward jest or sullen mock?"
"Mais non," said Ormond in a courtly tone.
"The Princess Gwendolyn, heir to the throne."

The tousled knight bowed feeling much chagrined.
Gwendolyn looked stern but inwardly grinned.
A knight, she thought, with a fair countenance;
That leads not to the way of abstinence.
In short, I fear I may lose my poor heart;

But prithee place the horse before the cart.
We have hard riding and a war to win
Else there be scant hope of Queen Gwendolyn.
I am in truth quite pleased to see him here.
The heavy odds we face are most severe,

And he can fight like a tiger uncaged -
Or a proud woman whom life hath enraged.
Yet his ways are not lacking in humor
Nor subtle charm. But court we not rumor.
Let us bank the fires of nascent feelings
And show ourselves wary in our dealings
Until we shall better test his mettle.
Does a fight alone show his fine fettle?
"Come, eager knight, let us be on our way;
I bid thee ride with Ormond this fine day."

The following day about mid-morning,
Trumpets blared; and with no hint of warning,
Over a low hill thundered King John's knights,
Scattering small birds into screeching flights.
The air trembled with a deafening roar
As churning, pounding hooves towards them bore
A gut-wrenching charge with lances leveled.
Gwendolyn's troops stood as if bedeviled
Until the tousled knight was heard to shout:
"Charge smartly, comrades, or we face a rout!"

He and Princess Gwendolyn took the lead,
Followed by Pierre on his hot-blooded steed.
Her soldiers then let loose a rousing cry:
"For Princess Gwendolyn: conquer or die!"
But John's fast-charging forces reached them first;
And Ormond, wielding his sword, feared the worst.
The battle raged amidst shrill cries of pain;
Three youthful French knights were already slain.
Pierre was struck, and blood seeped from his shoulder;
He looked haggard and many years older.

Gwendolyn thrust her sword and pierced a throat;
Her dying foe shrieked like a slaughtered shoat.
She saw the tousled knight swing a huge mace,
Then turn round to her with an impish face:
"Most honored Princess, this be dreary work
And better left to the bloodthirsty Turk
Who separates with delight heads from necks,
Caring little if they be French or Czechs."
Confusion and disorder everywhere;
Groans and bellowed oaths in the dusty air;

Swords and battle-axes stained black with blood;
Exhausted faces marked with sweat and crud;
The grappling armies wildly writhed and churned
Like a speared monster to the deep returned.
Her troops fought valiantly to no avail;
Bit by bit, John's knights began to prevail.
They pushed the Princess towards a swift stream.
Flashing in the sun were silvery bream.
The racing waters would block a retreat;
And all would now end in bloody defeat.

Just as a crushing rout and chaos loomed,
A horn sounded; and Jonah's deep voice boomed:
"Attack! Attack! No weak-kneed mercy show!"
Jonah's troops dealt the King a stinging blow,
Attacking unseen from around the hill
And depriving John of his gory kill.
The heartless battle slowed its torrid pace.
John's weary knights showed not the slightest trace
Of eagerness the Princess to pursue
As she rallied her forces and withdrew.

The two armies camped at no great distance;
The morrow would bring a further instance
Of intense fighting and mortal struggle.
The Princess had no spare troops to juggle.
Her camp grew still as black night descended;

Sparks from the fires to Heaven ascended.
The jolly, fighting surgeon's task was grim
As he staunched wounds by the flickering, dim
Light of resin torches. Wild, piercing screams
Rent the night and would, like ghosts, haunt their dreams.

The worn Princess spoke in a somber voice
And asked her close friends what, if any, choice
They had but to fight on as best they could.
Their chances, she averred, were hardly good.
"But first: Annabelle, how goes our bold Pierre?"
"Pretty fair, Your Grace, he does passing fair
And ready to fight at the break of dawn
Unless the King's men are long up and gone."
"Ah, French wit. Your instincts, Ormond, were sound;
To Sarafina, we'll one day get round."

"And Your Grace drew the correct conclusion.
Jonah's charge was an inspired intrusion
Without which we would surely not be here,
Debating the next step in your career."
Gwendolyn looked from one to the other:
"Long have we lived and labored together.
Our mutual respect is built on trust;
To deceive is something we never must
Do. Outnumbered by at least two to one,
Tomorrow's battle will hardly be fun.

For myself, I have a pledge to fulfill.
Any man – or woman – for whom the chill
Breath of black, hovering Death draws too nigh
Should leave with no tear or remorseful sigh."
Her bleak words cast on them a heavy pall;
Annabelle shivered beneath her wool shawl.
William was the first to break the silence;
His words were soft but tinged with violence.
"First among us to hear Your Grace's creed,
I taught you the bow; you taught me to read.

A wandering scoundrel, you gave me hope;
I might, otherwise, have swung from a rope."
The arguing twins were the next to speak,
But with just one voice - neither brash nor meek:
"You found us shameful boys and made us men.
And though your thoughts are oft beyond our ken,
You offer plain justice to all alike.
For the Brave Maiden, we face lance or pike."

Annabelle spoke in a voice strong and clear:
"I have always held portrait painting dear,
But art is just so much useless rubbish
Where freedom and justice do not flourish.
I now have learned to fight as well as paint;
My resolve is sure and in no ways faint."
Bearded Jonah rose up to his full height
And exclaimed with the God of Jacob's might:
"My Princess, you welcomed an errant Jew
And refused to hate as so many do.

You need no statement of my loyalty,
Which is yours as plain maid or royalty.
Besides what this tinker loves most of all
Is a hearty fight and a rousing brawl."
"As much," laughed the Princess, "As poaching roe?"
Jonah nodded and watched the fire's hot glow.
"I am the last here to join this crusade,
But Your Grace one time hurried to my aid –
Not to forget your snarling, wolfish friend
Who saved us from a cruel, fiendish end.

Running has never been much to my taste;
And besides, this field is too good to waste.
They must charge us at a downwards angle.
Aiming from below will cause a tangle.
When that occurs, we will with swords wade in,"
Finished the tousled knight with a wide grin.
"We shall also place archers in yon copse

To attack their flanks and destroy their hopes,"
Added the Princess in a quiet way.
Ormond had something he wanted to say:

"Your officers are all of the same mind;
The troops, as well, I am sure you will find.
John's knights are trained in all facets of war,
But your fighters are trained – and one thing more:
They have a sacred cause for which they fight;
And of this factor, one should not make light.
I think it past time we all went to bed.
Enough is known, and enough has been said."
"Thank you, noble Ormond, and all the rest.
Tomorrow God metes out a fearsome test.

Our intention is not to harm the King,
But above all he must see this one thing:
A king rules always for the common weal
And thus must neither tyrannize nor steal.
Victorious, we impose the charter;
Beaten, our lives are not worth a garter.
Go ye now; rest in whatsoever style
Ye may. Pray let me walk alone awhile."
The Princess moved about in plain attire
And left encouragement at every fire.

A young peasant woman newly arrived
Asked all too earnestly wherefore they strived.
"We fight for justice, peace and rights for all -
No matter whether they be great or small.
This looming battle sets for us a course
That to lose will bring ages of remorse."
Her words caused sighs and murmurs of assent.
She kept on under God's broad firmament
And sat on a hardwood stump deep in thought.
Sarah lay beside the fresh stump and caught
Her mood. Gwendolyn recalled as a child
The first time her knightly father beguiled

Her with a little, wooden sword. She held
It fast in her fist and years later felled
In a tourney, a seasoned knight - first of
Many. She gazed at sparkling stars above
And thought of stories a magician told
Of myriad creatures from planets cold
As ice and boiling hot – all far removed
From earth and on mankind greatly improved.

Strange, but any stranger than here below?
At which point, the black night began to glow.
I wonder, she thought, if tomorrow eve,
I'll see these bright stars and so calmly breathe.
The elfin Queen and King now hovered near;
Sarah roughly growled and pricked up an ear.
The diaphanous Queen waved her slim wand
Over Sarah's head like a swaying frond.
The gray wolf lay her head between her paws
As sleep closed her eyes and slackened her jaws.

Father, Mother, I badly need your help;
I am little more than a wet-eared whelp.
Many on each side will tomorrow fall
Because I dared raise a clarion call.
By what fool's arrogant, out-jointed pride
Did I think to divert the rushing tide
Of men's affairs to a different course?
Arrayed against us is a mighty force,
The terrible power and panoply
Of high England. Do we stand fast or flee?

This heavy choice cannot be called a choice.
My counselors have spoken with one voice.
We have thus far made such noble progress
As would bid us advance and not regress.
Though I am proper heir and royal niece,
Dare I seek to capture the Golden Fleece?
Tomorrow I may stand next to the throne,

But tonight, I feel frightened and alone.
The elfin Queen then stretched out a finger,
Touched Gwendolyn's cheek but did not linger.

Yet I see before me only one road;
I am no timid sheep that needs a goad.
In such a worthy cause, how can we fail?
It will be John's wicked knights who turn tail.
She scratched the dozing wolf between the ears;
Tomorrow would come without doubts or tears.
As she walked back to camp, her mind at ease;
She noticed a strangely familiar breeze.
"Thank you, Father, the road ahead is straight.
Count Gerard, come meet, God willing, thy fate."

As dawn brushed the sky with pale, rosy streaks,
Both camps stirred; and as the warrior Greeks
Studied entrails for signs of yea or nay,
Clusters of anxious fighters knelt to pray.
Every soldier to the same God appealed
With a cross here and there upon a shield.
As their own God, each army laid a claim
And sought victory in his righteous name.
As Gwendolyn prayed, a thundering sound
Brought her troops to their feet and shook the ground.

Five score riders approached - weapons at rest.
They rode towards camp from the still dark west -
Five score knights led by a tall, craggy earl.
Many wore round their necks a handsome pearl.
Ormond's face broke into a wide-lipped smile:
"Owen of Harlech, you're always in style.
Your Grace, may I present our Welch allies.
When Owen promises, he never lies."
"All the border knights are welcome indeed;
The Welch have long suffered from King John's greed."

Owen replied: "I take your cause as mine;
Now may Heaven our destinies entwine."
From across the meadow, trumpets rang out.
All mounted fast and heard Gwendolyn shout:
"The moment of our great trial has come.
Let each one here add to the total sum
Of all our hopes and high expectancies.
Adamantine fate flings us on the seas
Of bloody combat. That, we must endure;
But take comfort, for victory is sure

If each man and woman play well their part.
Evil shall not conquer a valiant heart.
We have a noble cause for which we stand
And which we shall trumpet throughout the land.
Archers, fast to your protected places;
Victory will soon light up your faces.
Mounted troops, form your battle lines to charge.
We advance to a destiny writ large."
'Ere long the din of pounding hooves was heard.
Time, for an instant, stopped; and no one stirred.

Pennons flapping, horses at a dead run,
Their armor glinting in the morning sun,
The sight of the King's charge curdled the blood
As the meadow was trampled in a flood
Of foam-bedecked chargers and visored knights.
In the bright sky circled two keen-eyed kites -
Silent witnesses to the scene below
Where Death sharpened his scythe, and blood would flow.
John's galloping knights leveled sharp lances;
Gwendolyn and Ormond exchanged glances.

The King's army numbered five hundred strong.
"Charge!" cried the Princess as she spurred headlong
Into the path of the onrushing tide,
Greeting her fate like a dewy-eyed bride.
Owen and Ormond spurred forward as well.

In a flash was broken the fearful spell,
And her emboldened troops surged to the fore
As shouts of "Gwendolyn" rose in a roar.
A cloud of arrows whistled overhead
To claim the first of this day's many dead.

Will's archers again stretched their supple bows
And shot from the copse and behind hedgerows.
Wounded coursers screamed in pain and tumbled
While their fallen riders tripped and stumbled,
Gyved in their heavy, clanking suits of mail.
Death-dealing arrows fell like sheets of hail.
Up and down the meadow, the armies clashed.
Sparks flew from whetted swords, and maces crashed
Against bobbing helmets and plates of steel.
A callow knight began to slowly kneel

In the clutches of Death's unyielding grip,
Pierced through the stomach by a lance's tip.
His cold hands gripped the lance; his jaw was set
In a frieze of pain one would not forget.
All through the hot morning, the battle raged
As if two rival beasts had been uncaged.
Of defeat, all foresaw the consequence
And plied their grisly task with a vengeance.
Great gusts of wind disturbed the leaden air.
Blood-flecked, choking dust swirled everywhere.
Annabelle found it difficult to breathe
As she thrust and parried without reprieve.
Two hardened knights had she already killed.
Blood-stained her armor, her dry mouth was filled
With the sour taste of grime and ashen dust.
Her youthful eyes gleamed with the killing lust,
Which intemperate battle so enflames
That commonplace life seems but children's games
When justly weighed against the frenzied state
Of killing foes for whom Death will not wait.

Her quivering arms felt consumed with fire;
Her worn sword she could barely lift higher
Than her waist. Leaning against an oak tree,
Cruel Philip's attack she did not see.
Raising his sword to strike a blow most foul,
Philip just then heard a deep-throated growl
And turned in time to see a springing blur.
His last sensation was of fangs and fur
As Sarah neatly ripped his throat in two
And left his torn windpipe dangling askew.

"Sarah, that bit gave me a nasty fright,"
Patting the wolf as she rejoined the fight.
Unhorsed, the dogged twins fought back to back,
Each in turn with a mocking joke to crack.
"Lay on, ye simpering aristocrats;
We've brought steel enough for a dozen rats,"
Egbert laughed as he parried a quick thrust
By bluff Sir Roger who shouted and cussed:
"You bigmouthed peasant scum, I'll split your head
And make you wish you had stayed home abed."

So saying, a vicious riposte struck home;
Egbert sighed and sputtered thick blood and foam,
Collapsing wordless at his brother's feet.
His twin turned pale as a white linen sheet.
Howling like a vengeful Fury, Selwyn
Straddled the body of his fallen twin
And a studded mace so mightily swung
That he cracked Roger's ribs and pierced a lung.
The knight fell dying on top of Egbert;
The two bodies quivered, then lay inert.

Jonah ranged over the meadow at will,
Unhorsing knights with his brawn and great skill.
Stephen of Kent faced him in a duel
And met the fate of Philip the Cruel,
But not before his slashing sword cut deep.

Dark blood the ragged wound began to seep,
But brave Jonah fought on despite the cut
Until he fell off by a crofter's hut.
Riding near, the tousled knight saw him fall
And defended him against one and all.

Gwendolyn saw this by fortunate chance
And ordered two men, each armed with a lance,
To stand guard while his torn shoulder was bound.
Gallant Jonah staggered up from the ground
And unwisely sought to remount his steed,
But the deep wound began once more to bleed.
"Rest easy, valiant friend," cried Gwendolyn.
"This battle we will in short order win.
I feel God telling me the tide has turned;
The moment will soon come for which I've yearned."

Indeed, the King's forces were falling back
Under the pressure of her grim attack.
The foul Duke of Essex was seen to flee.
The High Constable strove desperately
To halt the collapse - but of little use.
First fear, then stark panic, was on the loose.
As the King's men began a headlong run,
Gwendolyn searched for that envenomed one
With whom she had yet to settle a score.
Suddenly, she heard a sneering voice: "Whore!"

And turned quickly to face Gerard's contempt
As he bore down in a craven attempt
To dispatch the Princess while unprepared.
For truth or a fair fight, he little cared.
She lifted her shield in the nick of time,
But the blow knocked her in the dust and grime.
She struggled to her feet, her leg in pain,
And barely caught hold of a hanging rein
As Gerard spurred his horse and galloped past.
Jerking the loose rein tight and holding fast,

She spun the horse around and spilled Gerard,
Who crashed to the blood-soaked ground swearing hard.
She waited patiently for him to rise,
Then lifted her bright sword up towards the skies
And brought it down in a broad, sweeping arc
That Gerard parried just shy of its mark.
He swung his sword in turn and struck her arm;
She cried out in pain which sparked great alarm
In the tousled knight who stepped to the fray.
Ormond touched his arm and commanded: "Nay!

"This is a fight she must win on her own.
There are some paths in life we tread alone."
Gerard then delivered a vicious thrust
That sent the Princess reeling in the dust.
He towered above her with sword raised high
And laughing, said "Wench, get ready to die."
As a mournful cry rose from stricken hearts,
She kicked him smartly in the nether parts
And rising, fiercely drove her sword beneath
His breastplate. He fell dying to the heath,

Her blade driven up from stomach to chest.
The quivering hilt came slowly to rest.
A trickle of dark blood flowed down his chin.
Gerard's final sight was of Gwendolyn
Standing triumphant with tears in her eyes
As she spoke familiar names to the skies.
Beside his dead body, she quickly knelt
And drew a crested dagger from his belt.

Epilogue

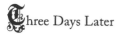hree Days Later

King John dispatched under a flag of truce
A high baron who offered no excuse
For the King's corrupt rule and England's state
But promised instead to negotiate.
In a field by a meandering brook,
Princess and uncle oaths of friendship took,
Then sat to talk at a rough-hewn table.
The King's barons wore cloaks fringed with sable.
The Princess appeared in humble raiment
But made her claim with a forceful statement.

"England is reeling from adversity.
She needs good laws, peace and prosperity:
A king who rules with impartial justice
And will banish every evil practice."
The charter she described in some detail.
As its meaning sunk in, the King turned pale.
She ended her speech with a quiet threat
That John should do nothing he might regret.
Gwendolyn allowed him some minor points,
Then rapped the table with her finger joints.

"If His Highness would be so good to sign,
We shall then repair to my camp to dine."
The High Constable watched with intense care
The Charter signed and Gwendolyn named heir.
All his elaborate schemes now vanished,
His high-flying aspirations banished.
But only, he thought, for the here and now
As his sullen mouth formed a silent vow
That he would in good time ascend the throne.
This thought he buried like a dog a bone.

As the Princess walked back towards her tent,
Two archers approached her with shoulders bent
Under the weight of a body they bore.
William, lying for three days at death's door,
Had just now relinquished his earthly shell
To answer the call of a distant bell.
With a seeping wound like a shallow pit,
Neither God nor the surgeon could seal it.
Day and night she had sought to comfort him,
Her eyes filling with tears up to the brim.

"Milady, pray you do not weep for me,
But send this body to my family.
Tell them I served God and a Princess well
And in raging battle was how I fell.
Tell them also how I had learned to read;
How from shameful ignorance was I freed."
She promised all of that and more besides;
Poverty no longer would tan their hides.
"By his royal and invested power,
John shall dub thee knight, my faithful archer.

As Sir William shall thou henceforth be known."
At these words, his shuttering eyes had flown
Open. In truth, each word now cost him dear:
"Thus honored, death I shall no longer fear."
She left his side only to meet the King
So was not there to hear his angels sing.
They shouldered him amidst silent weeping.
Peaceful, he appeared to her: just sleeping.
She softly bade them lay the body down
And garb it gently in a silken gown.

She requested Jonah to say a prayer
To entrust William to God's loving care.
For Egbert, Selwyn spoke in quiet tones,
Giving to the deep earth his flesh and bones.
He bade his spirit like a falcon soar

To watch over the Princess evermore.
All the dead were with solemn grace interred
While funeral masses and prayers were heard.
This doleful work, Thomas and John's priest shared;
No two less likely priests were ever paired.

Music that night through the camp resounded.
The fighters danced and in great leaps bounded
O'er flames. They sang in hearty unison
Without surcease until the morning sun
Brought healing sleep to aching bones and limbs.
Joined in merriment, hopeful peace begins
As the vanquished with victor celebrate;
And many encounter a worthy mate.
These proceedings, Flame looked at with dismay.
Will they so simply turn night into day?

She thought with a horse's cynical sense.
"For this peace to last, I'd not give tuppence!"
Gwendolyn and John watched with royal grace.
Ormond and Jonah had each a high place,
With knighthoods arranged by a future Queen.
Jonah's appetite was never more keen.
Painter again and Royal Treasurer,
Annabelle barely created a stir
By stating that she and Pierre planned to wed.
The Princess winked at her and dipped her head,

Asking the tousled knight with a shy grin:
"And who will wed poor Princess Gwendolyn?"
"Surely there be those with fortune and fame
Preceding a rude knight without a name."
"In this fabled land, I might garner both;
Yet to thee would I rather pledge my troth."
"And to thee do I freely give my love,
Sworn now before God and the stars above."
His words were greeted with a rousing cheer
As the Princess spoke softly in his ear:

"To whose name shall I murmur endearments
And swear my faith in holy sacraments?"
"Sir Hugh of Weatherford, my Brave Maiden,
Who shall be your husband and safe haven
Wherein ye shelter from the rude turmoil
That marks an honest monarch's ceaseless toil.
We shall have love, honor and progeny
To flatter thy wisdom upon thy knee."
"Never to me was such sweet love vouchsafed,
Nor my lonely heart so ardently chafed.

And thus my love to you I warmly give;
As man and wife, we shall forever live."
The elfin Queen now spread her gauzy wings
And hovered o'er head as a soft chime rings.
Elves and sprites in the spectral firelight danced;
Floating choirs sang, and mythic horses pranced.
Sarah calmly lifted her head to growl
As she heard in the woods a mournful howl.
Gazing raptly at a carpet of stars,
Gwendolyn's eye caught the red planet Mars.

Her thoughts now revolved around love and war;
To preserve the peace was a course she swore.
She thought of dear friends and family lost;
The cause was won but at a heavy cost.
She had traveled by a road long and hard
And not for a moment been off her guard.
She thought back to the very beginning.
In her ears, her Father's words were ringing:
"Honor and justice make a worthy cause;
Peace and prosperity need careful laws."

The journey begun as the merest child,
A Queen, from the cocoon, emerged and smiled.
"My Father would I lief see once again
To tell I have made my way among men –
And women." She felt then a gentle breeze

Touch her cheek and disappear in the trees.
As she gazed engrossed at the blazing fire,
She felt her spirits grow ever higher.